The Homesteader's Legacy

Tom watched Maria as Rigor's crony dragged her from her perch atop the wagon. She clung tightly to the cold metal bar that ran around the seat that was designed to keep the driver and his companions from sliding off.

"Come on," the man tugged at her. She kicked at him and clipped him in the chin. He fell to the ground. He had already pulled her past the edge of the seat. Maria was forced to cling to the seat rim and try to pull herself back up onto the top, or lose her grip and fall to the earth beside him.

The man cursed, got to his feet, and came back to grab her ankles and pull her the rest of the way off the wagon.

Tom fought the urge to step in. Smitty must have sensed he was about to move. Tom heard him click the hammer back on his pistol.

Maria continued to struggle, even though the man now had his arms wrapped tight around her waist and was dragging her to the horse. She flailed her arms and legs as hard as she could. She aimed to connect with another blow of her fists to his head before he could shove her up onto the horse.

Other Works From The Pen Of

Mary Jean Kelso

The Homesteader

Molly Kling lowered her rifle. Her aim was steady as she felt the trigger against her finger. Lead zinged inches from the stranger's left leg. No one was going to take what she had come for.

Goodbye Is Forever

When Lynne Garrett goes to visit her aunt in Virginia City, Nevada, she believes she's headed for a peaceful vacation in the picturesque old mining town. But then she unwittingly acquires a jeweled scarab necklace and finds herself being pursued by a menacing figure who will do anything to get it back. As she seeks to uncover the truth about the necklace, and her sinister pursuer, Lynne discovers that she's at the center of a complex scheme to save a stranger's life—by endangering hers.

The Homesteader's Legacy

by

Mary Jean Kelso

A Wings ePress, Inc.

Historical Romance Novel

Wings ePress, Inc.

Edited by: Leslie Hodges
Copy Edited by: Elizabeth Struble
Senior Editor: Leslie Hodges
Executive Editor: Lorraine Stephens
Cover Artist: Richard Stroud

Wings ePress Books
http://www.wings-press.com

Copyright © 2007 by Mary Jean Kelso
ISBN 978-1-59705-822-3

Published In the United States Of America

February 2007

Wings ePress Inc.
403 Wallace Court
Richmond, KY 40475

Dedication

For all my readers—

without you there would be no reason for the books.

One

A young girl's scream, a baby's wail, and a toddler's cry broke the quiet of the countryside near Moriarty, New Mexico. Although unheard by neighbors too distant to help, their voices screeched a heartrending cry.

Their mother lay writhing in pain in the dirt at their feet.

Only moments before, Molly Westerman had stood on the steps of her fine home, her eyes contentedly scanning her surrounding one hundred and sixty acres of farmland.

It had been a challenge to reach this level of success. She was proud of the work the whole family had done to make their dream come true.

She'd smiled as she'd looked at the windmill's blades spinning in the hot afternoon breeze. They'd reminded her of the day her husband, Trace, had come into their lives. At first, she had thought him a drifter, up to no good—untrustworthy. Later, she had thought her heart would burst with happiness when she learned their love was mutual.

Two of her stepchildren, from her first marriage, Rosie and Seth, were busy with chores nearby: Rosie, behind her, rocked baby Jacob in the cradle his proud father had made him. Eight-year-old Seth piled firewood beneath the big black kettle so Molly could make lye soap. Little Emmy, Molly and Trace Westerman's first born, clung to her mother's skirts as they watched Molly's eldest stepson, Andy, ride his beautiful black horse, Comet, along the back fence line. The variegated gray and white dog, Crazy Leg, bounded behind, barely out of reach of Comet's back hooves.

Life could not get much better than this, Molly had thought happily.

Then, she clutched her chest and lurched forward, falling from the front porch steps and landing on her knees in the soft dirt before her.

"Ma! What's wrong?" Rosie shrieked.

Emmy cried out as her mother's forward movement dragged the toddler, whose fists were entwined in the fabric of her bright yellow skirt, to the ground with her where she lay now, face down in the good earth.

The pain in Molly's chest was like a bullet ripping through her flesh and she gasped trying to catch her breath and wondering if she had been shot.

What is wrong?

Molly's palms were on the ground and she clutched her fingers into the granular soil trying to withstand the pain.

"Ma!" Rosie screamed again, as she ran to Molly's side.

Her shrill voice, when she saw Molly's graying face, hurt Jacob's ears. Jacob screwed his face into a scowl and began howling. Emmy, already frightened by the fall, and crying, raised her voice louder in the mourning chorus.

Seth, having run to stand alongside Molly's now prone body, stood, silently staring at her in disbelief.

Where is Pa? Rosie wondered as she moved to try to

right Molly from the ground.

She stopped shrieking, for the children's sakes, but the two babies still wailed while she tugged at Molly's arms to turn her on her back.

There was no color in Molly's face, now. Rosie held her fingers beneath Molly's nose and felt no breath. She drew her hand back slowly and began to sob, stuffing one fist into her mouth to stop the horrid sound before she alarmed the babies even more.

Trace, drawn from his workshop in the barn by the ruckus, ran at full speed past Molly's brilliant hollyhocks near the kitchen window and around the corner of the house. He skidded to a halt when he saw the scene before him, then dropped to his knees at Molly's side.

He took her arms, gently, and lifted her, leaning her shoulders across his thighs where he knelt in the soft dirt.

She wasn't breathing.

He felt the vein in her neck for a pulse.

He felt none.

Molly's dead! His mind didn't want to grasp the meaning of the words.

He wanted to beat the ground with his fists. He let his head drop backward and his eyes stared straight up toward the sky as if he was searching for an answer there.

God! How could You do this? He gritted his teeth and felt the pain throughout his body. How would he live without Molly? She, and the children, had become his whole life. *The children.* Concern for them, over that for himself, surfaced from the deep well of his grief.

"Rosie," he spoke quietly when he found his voice once more, "take Emmy and the baby inside and try to calm them. I'll take care of Molly."

"But, she's de——," Rosie broke off and blubbered.

Trace put a big arm around the girl and held her close to him. Her head reached only to his first rib and he held her tighter than was comfortable for her.

Rosie was soon to be eleven and, for such a tiny person, he sensed a big job lay ahead of her.

"I know. But, let's not upset the babies any more."

Tears burned behind his eyelids, but he tried to hold his emotions in check to reassure the children.

As he comforted Rosie, he remembered Molly running to greet him when he had returned from Texas to marry her. He could still see, in his mind, the sunshine yellow of her skirt whipping behind her as she ran down the drive toward him. He saw the wide smile across her lips as she tried to run and breathe at the same time. He could still feel the warmth of her body in his arms as he embraced her. He looked down at her face, now, as her features grew more ashen with every second.

Molly's determined spirit was somewhere else now.

"Go, Rosie. Take care of the little ones," he said in a scratchy voice.

Trace bent once more to Molly's side. This time he scooped his arms beneath her shoulders and knees. When he began to lift her, a gush of air rose from her mouth.

Was it the pressure of his arms against her back which caused her lungs to expel a final breath?

Rosie picked up baby Jacob's cradle. She positioned it against one hip and held it there with her arm wrapped around the wooden frame. With her free arm she reached out for Emmy's hand and led her inside the house.

Quickly, Trace laid Molly back on the ground and felt for a pulse. His calloused fingers sensed nothing. He moved them to the side of her neck. Pressing gently against the main artery, he held still and waited a second. Then, two seconds. At last, a faint beat pressed back against his fingertips.

Molly groaned slightly.

"Rosie," he called out toward the open front door, "she's still alive. Run quickly and send Andy for the doctor."

Trace knelt beside Molly again. Gently, he scooped his arms beneath Molly shoulders and legs once more. Trace rose to his feet with Molly in his arms. He carried her carefully into the house. He climbed the stairs, sideways, to the bedroom to avoid banging Molly's head against the wall.

He laid her on the patchwork cover on the big bed in their room. He straightened her skirt and untangled the fine strands of her long red hair, to lie alongside her face. He thought of the many happier nights they had spent in that same bed. He dropped to his knees onto the crocheted rag rug on the floor beside the metal-framed bed.

"Molly, can you hear me?"

He grabbed her wrist and felt for the pulse. It was stronger, now.

He kissed Molly's hand, dampening its calluses with tears before laying it down across her waist. *Whatever had happened could occur again.* He laid his head on his arms atop the patchwork cover next to Molly. There, he let his own tears flow. Wracked by sobs he didn't want the children to hear, he moved to the window and lifted it in the hope the sounds he made would pierce the air outside instead of bringing the children to the room.

When he finally turned, he saw Andy standing in the open doorway staring at Molly.

Andy's eyes looked searchingly at Trace's sullen face.

"She's alive, barely. Her heart must have stopped," Trace said simply, though he couldn't understand how someone with so much love in her heart could have it quit so suddenly and at such a young age.

"Hurry and get Doc Landry. I'll do what I can, but I don't know how much that will be."

Stunned, Andy turned away.

She can't die. She was the one to hold the family together when Pa died. She can't die. He hesitated in the doorway and leaned his forehead against the wall, fighting back tears. Then he spun around and burst down the stairs, through the kitchen and out the front door.

He leaped onto Comet's bare back.

They hit the main road at maximum speed as Andy urged the horse on. Maybe if they ran fast enough he could outrun this fear he felt inside. Maybe Doc Landry could do something for Molly if he hurried.

When Trace came back downstairs to the kitchen, Seth and Rosie were feeding Emmy a slice of the coarse bread Molly had baked the day before. They spread thick butter across its top and sprinkled it with sugar and cinnamon. Occasionally, Seth helped himself, to Emmy's frown of dismay.

Quickly, Trace grabbed a clean flour sack towel and the bucket of water sitting on the table. He hurried back upstairs.

Rosie watched him go with a worried furrow across her

brow. She felt as if she couldn't breathe—like someone was squeezing the air out of her lungs and holding on tight so it couldn't go back where it belonged.

~ * ~

On the road to Moriarty, Andy ran Comet until the horse was winded, then slowed him gradually to let him catch his breath.

Once he could push the horse onward again, he urged Comet to race full-speed down the main street of the little town and up to Doc Landry's office door. He guided the horse onto the wooden sidewalk as he shouted out, "Doc! Come quick. We need your help!"

Outside the doctor's office, he saw Nellie, Doc's horse, hitched to the buggy and the ends of the leather traces wound snug around the brake handle.

"What is it, Andy?" Doc asked as he opened the door. He wiped his hands on a towel as he leaned outside to see what all the commotion was about.

"It's Ma. Trace says her heart stopped. He says she's alive, but just barely."

Doc reached behind the door for his old black leather medical bag and ran for the buggy.

"Coming, Andy?"

"I'll be there soon."

Andy rode along slowly, letting Comet catch his breath after the hard ride to town. His reasoning mind told him he would have to go back as quickly as possible. *The younger kids will need me.* But, he had to clear his own head, first. He was confused by feelings of fear, hurt, anger and grief that terrified him. The possibility of losing Molly was more than he could comprehend and he stalled, slowing the horse gradually until, finally, he stopped still in the middle of the road.

He studied the town of Moriarty. It wasn't much, but there were people here. Live people. Rebecca Waite lived a few feet beyond a small clump of bushes in her parent's house behind the dry goods store.

Going on sixteen, Andy had felt the stirrings of romance inside his gut when they were together. He had walked her home from school many times and a couple of times they'd met in her father's barn and talked while relaxing in the hay. He well remembered staring into the soft blue of her eyes, their color less intense than most.

He remembered the sweet smell of the winter's hay and how it caught like thistledown in Rebecca's long blond curly hair when they lay across its soft bed.

He urged Comet on toward the Waite's back door as he wiped his face on his sleeve to clear up any remaining dust and tears.

"Becky," he called out when he reached the back yard.

He dismounted and moved closer to the small porch, holding Comet's reins until he could tie them to a bush by the step.

"Becky," his voice crackled. He cleared his throat and called a bit louder.

The back door opened and a pretty girl, near his age, poked her head outside. She smiled, then pulled her well curved lips straight when she saw Andy's distraught face

"Andy, what is it? What's wrong?"

"Can you come out for a bit?"

"I'll be back soon," Becky called to her mother. She let the door slam shut behind her and hurried down the steps toward Andy.

They turned toward the barnyard and both walked solemnly.

"Ma might die," Andy told her.

"Oh, no!" Becky replied, "That's terrible. What wrong with her?"

"Trace says her heart stopped beating, or something," Andy spoke fighting back the tears that threatened to spill. He did not want to cry in front of Becky! He was so close to being a man—he was determined to control himself. He cleared his throat again.

"Pa got her breathing again. I went for Doc Landry and he's headed out to examine her."

"That's so sad. What can I do to help?"

"I don't know that there's anything anyone can do. I've got to get back. The kids will need me."

"I'm so sorry. I'm sure my mother will fix some food and bring it over. Maybe I can help with the babies. Please, Andy, let me know what to do."

She turned quickly and kissed him on the cheek.

Andy bolted away before his tears spilled again.

Becky stood staring after him, feeling despair at his pain and remembering the softness of fuzz, from newly forming whiskers on his cheek, against her lips.

Andy was still "wet behind the ears," her father had told her. He still had "peach fuzz" on his face instead of whiskers.

She knew he hadn't said those things to hurt her. It was his way of teasing her and reminding her they were both too young to be serious about each other yet.

Her heart ached for Andy in his grief. She liked Molly.

It saddened her to know the teacher who had been good to her might no longer be there when she needed someone to talk to.

"Ma!" Rebecca shouted as she ran to the kitchen to give her mother the bad news. Becky knew her mother would organize the ladies of Moriarty to see that the family was fed and taken care of in their time of need. Taking care of people was what her mother did best.

As Andy reached the turn into the lane to the farm, Doc Landry was already climbing back into his buggy. Trace stood alongside. Andy stopped Comet beside them. The two men's voices were quiet as they discussed Molly's prognosis away from the younger children.

Doc shook his head.

"I can't say there'll be any change, Trace. I'd prepare for the worst and hope for the best. That's about all you can do."

Trace stared at the ground watching a small trail of ants carry their burdens in a line from the front porch toward the ragtag grass in the center of the driveway. He was aware the children in the house were watching through the window for any reaction to tell them if their mother would live or die.

Doc continued. "I think you were right. It probably was her heart. I gave her some medicine that might help. Be sure you get it down her morning, noon and night. If she improves, you can cut back to once a day after that. But, you'll need to see she stays on it every day from now on. Another bout of this and she might not come back. Frankly, it'll be a miracle if she makes it through the night."

Trace nodded.

Doc glanced at Andy with a sympathetic look. He called "gee" to Nellie and the buggy pulled out of the Westerman's yard leaving Trace and Andy standing with forlorn expressions on their faces in the buggy wheel's light stirring of dust.

Trace and Andy went into the house. Trace moved upstairs to Molly's bedside. Andy reached down and picked Jacob up from his cradle where he fussed.

"You and Seth go on outside for a bit. I'll watch Jacob and Emmy," Andy told the two anxious children.

After briefly checking on Molly, Trace reappeared in the kitchen.

He put a large hand on top of Emmy's head and felt her silken hair against his rough palm. He tousled the curls mindlessly.

"Andy, she's not doing well. Maybe it's the medicine, but she's in a deep sleep. I'm going to need to depend on you to stay at Molly's side. Keep her cooled down with the wet towel. Give her medicine to her with a spoon, just like Doc said. Make the younger kids stay downstairs until they go to bed so they don't disturb Molly.

"I'll try to be back by dark. If I don't make it back while it's still daylight, you'll have to leave her a bit to see that the chores are done before nightfall. Have Rosie watch her then. Once you're through with chores, come into the house and keep the door barred. Understand?"

"Yes, sir."

Trace dreaded leaving Andy to face the possibility that Molly might die in his charge while he was away. It was nothing any youngster should have to face. Doc had been adamant about the possibilities. Trace knew he must prepare a place for her, in case she didn't survive. Her chances to live were as good with Andy caring for her as they were with him. He knew Andy would follow his instructions. He couldn't send the boy out to do the job he had to do—with the threat of wild animals and outlaws—where he had to do it.

When Rosie and Seth saw Trace come out on the porch with his hat in his hand, it was a sure sign that he was headed somewhere.

"Is Molly in her room?" Rosie asked as she approached timidly.

"Yes. Andy is going to take care of her. Keep Jacob and Emmy in your room tonight, if I don't get back by bedtime, Rosie. Seth, you can stay there, too."

Seth looked up at Trace with large, frightened eyes. He wove one of Crazy Leg's soft ears between the fingers on one hand. The dog sat patiently waiting for Seth to play with him.

"It'll be all right. I promise. I'll do my best to be back before you go to sleep."

Trace went to the barn to get tools and saddle his horse, Lucky.

"Whoa, boy," he spoke to the animal when it balked at carrying the short handled shovel Trace held in his hand. The horse had thrown him many times before when he had called him by the name Flapjack and he wasn't in the mood for a toss right now. He had work to do and the animal would simply have to obey.

It had been Molly's idea to rename the horse with the hope of giving him a better disposition under a milder mannered title. So, Lucky he became because Molly had told Trace they were "lucky" the two of them had come into their lives.

Now, if Doc's prognosis was right, he had to prepare a grave for Molly. If they got their miracle—well, he'd pray for that while he worked.

Trace eased into the saddle and shifted the shovel, trying to figure out how he could carry the tool he needed and still stay on the sometimes-cantankerous horse. He pulled the rifle from its scabbard and inserted the shovel, handle down, in its place. He laid the rifle across his lap near the saddlehorn. He eased the horse out of the stall, through the barn door and outside into the sunshine.

As he passed the house, he saw two apprehensive faces staring at him from the open front door.

"Mind what I said," he told Rosie and Seth. "Listen to Andy and take care of the babies."

He saw their heads nod. He knew he could trust Rosie to look after the little ones.

He nudged Lucky down their roadway and toward the main road. There, he turned left and urged the horse into a trot toward the far off mountain where he and the family had first met.

~ * ~

Trace neared the mountain and found the desired trail that led to the outcropping of rocks where he had first seen Molly Kling and her three step-kids. Besides the homestead, it had always been Molly's favorite area. It was the location where they had gathered rocks for their home's foundation. It was the site where they had come for picnics and fun. It was a fitting place for Molly.

The nearly four years in-between that day, when they first met and now had been filled with happiness making the time seem too short. He was bitter that God might take Molly so soon. They had so much more life to share, if only Fate wouldn't play its cruel joke on them.

Trace swung his long legs down from the saddle. When he stood beside the horse, he stretched. He had pushed Lucky as hard as he figured he could without bringing him up lame and the ride had been rougher on his own body than he had anticipated.

He checked the cinch to be sure it hadn't loosened before he pulled the shovel from the scabbard and replaced the rifle. In the past, Lucky had been known to rear and buck Trace off if his cinch allowed the saddle to twist. Trace gave the belt an extra tug for good measure. He led Lucky to a small tree where he tied him beneath taller trees.

"Now, don't give me any foolishness, Lucky. I've got work to do and I don't feel like tracking down a horse that tugs itself loose and wanders off."

Trace set about selecting a site for Molly's grave.

When he found a suitable space, he stood where the head of the hole would be and looked between the tree trunks out toward the valley floor. If he had extra good eyesight, he could make out the house from there. As it was, there was a light mark on the landscape where he judged the house and farmland to be. He set about digging, concentrating on the pieces of slate he had to pick out and lay aside. He would situate them as a cover on top, when the final time came.

Trace worked feverishly, trying to beat the curtain of darkness he knew would soon fall. He knew he would not—could not—sleep this night.

He had buried too many people he loved in his short lifetime of thirty-five years. For a moment thoughts of his own parent's graves flashed through his mind as he remembered them on the hill above the old T-bar-W ranch back in Texas.

Finally, he decided his work here, on this lonely mountainside, was done.

He prayed he would not have to fill the grave—that Molly's tough, resilient character would prevail—that God would give them at least a few more years of happiness together.

A clap of thunder rolled across the sky. He looked up to see a bolt of lightning flash as a black cloud moved overhead. The dark underbelly ripped open and torrential rain dumped, like water poured from a bucket, over his head. Then pellets of sleet drummed on him and Lucky. The horse moved his legs nervously. His eyes searched for protection from the ice, but his reins held him where he was.

The rain fell in torrents, causing rivulets of muddy water to run down the pile of dirt Trace had just dug from the mountain. Mud washed against his boots. He hurried to untie Lucky and mount the horse, leaving the shovel stuck in the top of the dirt pile for the upcoming job tomorrow or whenever it was necessary.

Before Trace could situate his posterior in the saddle, comfortably, the downpour soaked through his clothes and, soon, had his skin as wet as the horse's hide. Whichever way he tilted his head to block the rain and sleet, cold water ran from the brim of his hat, at its lowest level, and dumped down his shirt and pants.

It was growing even darker with the storm and coming nightfall.

Then, as fast as it had come, the storm moved on and sunshine lit the mountainside once more.

Trace guided Lucky's reins to pick his way, carefully, off the slick mountain trail and headed toward the flatter wagon road leading to the farm and Moriarty. He looked back and could still see the open grave on the slant of the mountain. He pressed his knees into Lucky's sides. If he hurried back to the barn, he could have Molly's coffin built before the children awoke in the morning. He felt a chill run down his cold back. He hoped the sun would soon dry his clothes and warm him in the short time he had before dark.

He swatted the horse's rump with the end of the reins. Lucky reared back, surprised at the bite of the leather. His eyes widened and he moved to toss Trace off his back. His rear feet slid on the slick mud and he was forced to drop his front legs to keep from falling.

Trace realized his mistake instantly. He was glad he had tightened the cinch.

"Whoa, Boy. There's no point in me taking my hurt out on you!" He reached back and rubbed the area where the leather had snapped against the horse's flesh, trying to soothe the animal.

"I won't do that again, I promise."

If Lucky didn't retaliate, again, and no other danger lay between the mountain and the farm, he just might make it home in time to finish the job ahead.

Two

Early the next morning, when Rosie awoke, several neighbors were camped out in their front yard. Anxious to be of assistance to the trouble-stricken family, the women had brought food to prepare and were working silently in the kitchen so as not to wake the children.

The men milled about outside near their wagons. They were waiting for Trace to give them the sign that he had finished his woeful task of building the wooden casket and needed their help to carry it.

Rosie slipped quietly from her bed so as not to wake Seth or the babies. The door to Molly's room was open and Andy dozed with his head resting across his folded arms on the edge of her bed. A woman, who had assisted Doc Landry with other patients, now kept watch at Molly's bedside, letting Andy sleep. Rosie padded past them on bare feet and down the stairs to the kitchen.

Mrs. Waite was the first to see her and she reached out to the girl and clutched Rosie close.

"You poor youngun'," she said as she touched Rosie's sleep-tussled hair.

Rosie felt the tears she had held tight through the night

release and she wept uncontrollably.

Mrs. Waite knelt to Rosie's height, then sat on the floor and held the girl's slight frame on her lap.

"There, there. You go ahead and cry it all out. We're going to see you get through this. Becky, get the child a glass of water, please."

Becky moved to do as she was asked.

Soon, Andy came down the stairs in sleep-crumpled clothes. He had kept watch not only on Molly the evening before, while Trace was gone, but when he found Rosie, in her room worried and unable to sleep, he had cradled Jacob in his arms as well. Rosie had been exhausted from fighting to get Jacob settled down for the night and leaned against the wall, holding watch over Seth and the babies. Andy had comforted her as best he could and when she finally joined Emmy and Seth in sleep, he had rocked Jacob in Molly's rocker. Andy tilted his head back and stared at the ceiling late into the night. At some point, Jacob slept and Andy was able to settle him into his cradle near Rosie.

He had heard Trace return to the barn and what few dozes he captured the rest of the night came between the staccato sound of Trace's hammering. Every rap, he knew, was a nail in Molly's coffin. He wondered how she slept with the banging surely telling her how poor her chances were.

At daybreak he heard the wagons creak into the yard, the hammering cease for a while and then begin again.

Groggy, still, from the long night, Andy made his way toward the aroma of fresh-brewed coffee.

He saw Becky, neatly dressed with a fresh white

starched apron tied around her waist, standing in their kitchen filling a glass with water from a pitcher.

He felt slovenly and unfit. But, she seemed not to notice.

"Good morning, Andy," she spoke as if nothing were amiss.

"Morning, Becky, Mrs. Waite."

Mrs. Waite was helping Rosie to the kitchen table, now, and took the glass from Becky's hand.

"Becky, do pour Andy some coffee. Once Rosie is settled, I'll stir up some flapjacks. I'm sure everyone is probably starving."

It had taken longer than Becky had hoped for the neighbors to get things together and travel to the Westerman homestead. She had planned to bring some of her mother's fried chicken to the family in time for supper the night before, but the time had passed quickly as they prepared to set out.

Rosie, Emmy and Seth had made do with cold meat and bread and butter. Little Jacob, used to being nursed, had finally given in to one of Emmy's old weaning bottles when his frustration and hunger would let him hold out no longer.

"I'll go get the babies," Becky offered as the soft wail of Emmy's voice called "Mama."

"I'll carry Jacob's cradle down," Andy said.

They moved up the stairs, without conversation, and drew nearer to the soft wailing.

Emmy, sitting in the middle of Rosie's big comforter, looked curiously at Becky when she and Andy entered the small room. Jacob stirred in his sleep, causing the cradle to rock.

The odor of urine was in the air and Andy noted, mentally, that they would have to open the window and hang Rosie's bedding out to dry as Emmy had surely wet it.

"Hi, Emmy, remember me?" Becky asked the toddler. She reached to take the child from the warmth of the covers. "I'll help you downstairs."

Andy grasped Jacob's cradle by the slotted foot and headboard, sticking his fingers through the holes Trace had carved in each end for that purpose. The weight of the bed and the baby was more than he could carry comfortable and he immediately moved toward the stairs.

"I swear I don't know how Rosie carts this thing around. Sometimes I think she's stronger than me."

"Probably just practice," Becky assured him.

"Mama?" Emmy asked.

"No, Sweetie. But, Rosie's downstairs. Want to see Rosie?"

Emmy stared at the girl carrying her. *Where is my Mama? Why am I in the arms of someone I don't know?* But, the person seemed to know how to carry her so the ride was comfortable and she didn't complain, simply stared at her.

When Andy sat the cradle on the floor, Rosie came over to check on Jacob. The move had not disturbed him and hunger had not yet awakened him.

"Andy, breakfast is ready," Mrs. Waite said.

"I'm not hungry—thank you," he added. "I have to milk the cow. Please let someone else have it."

"All right, then. I'll feed the children and we'll save

some for you when you're finished with the milking," she said with a persistence he knew he could not refuse. She stood looking after him, with a plate stacked high with steaming flapjacks in her hand.

He grasped the bail of the milk bucket and started out the door toward the barn.

Mrs. Waite looked at her daughter and shook her head.

"He's going to be a difficult one to keep healthy, if he doesn't eat regularly," she advised her daughter.

"Momma! That's none of my concern."

Mrs. Waite looked at the other women. Two of them ducked their heads together and snickered. Mrs. Waite rolled her eyes toward the ceiling.

Is it that obvious I'm smitten with Andy Kling?

"Well, it isn't. Besides, Ma, now's not the time to be funnin' me." *Not with his stepmother lying nearly dead upstairs*, she wanted to say, but stopped to avoid upsetting the younger children.

"Andy's just a hard worker. And, that's good—isn't it?"

"Yes," they all agreed, that was a good trait in a man.

The women busied themselves dishing up plates for the men outside and delivering them to their respective husbands before joining the children back inside and eating their own morning meal.

They, then, set about doing the household chores while they waited for Molly Westerman's fate to be decided.

Trace was finishing the last bevel on the edge of the casket when Andy entered the barn.

He was haggard and exhausted.

Andy raised the pail up. "Bossy needs milking," he

said for lack of any other words.

Trace nodded. He rubbed his palm across the final board, his thoughts taking him to other times, other places. Even he didn't know how he would get through his next few responsibilities. But, he must.

He moved past Andy, laying a heavy hand on the boy's shoulder as he passed.

"I checked on Molly earlier. You did a good job watching over her."

"She hasn't woke up, yet."

"I know. Doc said the medicine would keep her under to give her heart a chance to rest and repair itself. She made it through the night. That's a good sign, according to Doc."

Andy wondered. *Just where is the critical line between life and death?* He'd done what he was told but he knew it was something that was in God's hands—not his.

Trace moved to the open barn door to ask someone to help carry the casket to the back of the buckboard for now.

"I'll go tell the wife to get the children where they won't see anything and ask questions," Becky's father said.

"Thanks."

The men waited until they saw Rosie and Becky carrying the babies toward the windmill and the shelter of the high-strung hops on the morning side of the garden.

Mrs. Waite had pointed out the tallest hiding spot on the property. Becky carried Jacob while Rosie led Emmy by the hand and they headed for the shade to play. Once they were there, their view of the front yard would be obstructed by the hop vines climbing the tall wires. Trace and the men could set the casket in the buckboard and cover it with a tarp.

No point in causing more concern for the younger kids, Trace thought.

When she knew that the children were occupied, Mrs. Waite carried a basin of warm water to Molly's room to wash the earth Molly so loved from her face and hands. She combed the particles of dirt from her hair and, with the help of the two other women, she removed Molly's blouse and bright yellow skirt that had billowed in the wind the day Trace returned from Texas. They found a fresh nightgown and dressed her limp body.

"There," Mrs. Waite said with satisfaction. "She should be much more comfortable. Do you need someone to spell you, Susan?"

"No, I'm fine. She seems to be resting easier and it's nearly time to give her more medicine. I'll call you if I need to leave even for a moment."

As Mrs. Waite moved through the door, she met Trace in the hallway. He carried long stalks of Molly's beloved red hollyhocks in a container of water.

"Any change?"

"She seems to be resting easier," Susan, the woman at Molly's bedside repeated.

He moved to the bed and sat the flowers on the table alongside.

"I'll go on down and get some coffee, myself," Susan said, giving him some time alone with his wife as she followed Mrs. Waite.

Trace lifted Molly's limp hand and held it tightly

between his two rough palms. There was warmth in her hand and, although she didn't wake up, he noted a slight stir of her head.

"Trace," Doc Landry greeted him as he walked through the door.

"She's still with us, Doc."

"Good. She made it through the night. That's always optimistic."

Doc busied himself checking Molly.

"She seems to be responding to the medicine. Cut the dose in half now and she should start coming around. Try to get some broth or something nourishing down her."

"When will we be out of the woods, Doc?"

"It's hard to say. I expect, in a few days, she should be more alert. Don't rush her. Keep her down and don't let her start moving around too soon. I'm going to keep checking back every day to see how she's doing." Doc snapped his black bag closed.

"You know Molly, if I don't keep her sedated, she'll overdo it as soon as she has the energy to get up. Any chance of her body repairing the damage could go right out the window..."

~ * ~

It was days before Molly finally was awake for long enough intervals to sit up and take nourishment. She began to gradually rebuild her strength.

The townspeople went back to their own lives and left Molly in Trace's care. Her recovery would take a long while, Doc Landry had told the group, once Molly's health began to turn around.

School started and a substitute performed Molly's

teaching duties while she remained confined to her room.

Trace continued to sleep on a pad on the floor in their room at night in order to watch over Molly, yet not disturb her rest. He rose and checked on her throughout the night. Apprehension hung heavy within him. He would sacrifice whatever was necessary, if Molly would just live. With each passing day, Molly gradually became stronger and it appeared God might relent and let her remain with her family.

Each day, when Trace heard the stirrings of the youngsters in the bedrooms nearby, he arose tired and listless.

Jacob was crawling now. His cradle would soon be put away, but Trace couldn't bear to part with it. His hands had put so much love and hope into the shaping of the wooden cradle that he and Molly had dreamed would hold several children before its retirement. He stalled off the time that he would have to remove it to storage. Now, he wondered if Molly's health would ever allow her to have another child, without risking her life again. Jacob could be the last baby to sleep in the cradle. He'd let him continue to sleep there a while longer before he built a new bed for Emmy and they moved Jacob to the crib.

~ * ~

A heavy pall hung over the Kling/Westerman homestead. Winter came and went and when Molly's hollyhocks began to grow outside the kitchen window, again, Molly was finally able to make her way downstairs.

"Don't fuss so, Trace," Molly pleaded as he held her elbow tight with his cupped hand to assist her to the rocking chair that had been moved to sit next to the fireplace.

When she sat down, Emmy scrambled onto her lap despite Trace's efforts to keep her at bay.

Jacob crawled to Molly's feet and Trace lifted him into his arms.

Molly smiled. "It's good to be part of the family again."

Her recovery had been slow, causing Trace to wonder, at times, if it would be complete.

Did Molly survive only to remain an invalid?

"Trace Westerman, get that look off your face," the fire of the old Molly chided him.

"What look?"

"You know! I am better. I get stronger every day now. Save the hang dog look for someone else."

Trace chuckled.

"Right!"

"Haven't we withstood worse?"

"Nothing could have been worse than losing you. You really gave us a scare."

"But, I'm here. Next fall I'll be teaching, again." Molly spoke with determination. "You might not let me work in the garden this year, but you can't keep me shut inside forever. Now, take these two and let's go sit in the sunshine."

The world was warming now, and the end of the school year would soon be at hand. Molly's replacement schoolteacher had kept the kids busy during the winter and with Rosie, Seth and Andy in school all day, Trace was left at home to care for Molly and the two babies until the three older children came back at night.

Although he enjoyed keeping Molly and the babies company during the day, he sometimes felt like a caged animal that had just found freedom when he could turn the little one's care over to Rosie and Seth when they rode in from school. He and Andy would then busy themselves with outside chores.

Crazy Leg bounded along beside the two of them on the days when Seth couldn't find a way to entice Emmy outside.

This particular afternoon, Trace released the babies to Rosie and helped Molly upstairs to rest before he and Andy set about their chores. Outside, Crazy Leg ran barking back and forth between the barn and the fence dividing the pasture from the garden plot.

"What's wrong with you, boy?" Andy asked as the dog barked again, snapping the air with his teeth and charging back to the fence.

"We better go see what's bothering him," Trace said. "Let me get my rifle in case it's a snake or rodent."

When Trace and Andy reached the fence, the bottom wire showed signs of having been stretched and tufts of dog hair clung in the barbs where Crazy Leg had forced his way beneath its taut line.

"Something's sure got him riled up," Trace told Andy.

"I haven't seen him act like this since the time he was after that old rattler," Andy agreed.

The dog wriggled his way beneath the wire again and bounded a few feet ahead of the two of them before stopping to look back and plead for Trace and Andy to follow.

"*Bark! Bark!*"

"We're coming," Trace said as he held the bottom wire down with the rifle butt and then pinched the two top strands together so Andy could climb between them and the bottom wire.

The dog jumped to his feet from where he lay waiting in the pasture, and bounced across the grass. He followed the trail by scent and looked back to see that his humans continued to stay on track.

Trace and Andy were running, now, in an attempt to keep up with Crazy Leg.

"Must—not—be—a snake," Trace said breathlessly.

Andy concentrated on the landscape ahead. Crazy Leg was about halfway between them and a dark lump. Andy could see it sticking above the grass like a small boulder. He looked quizzically at Trace. *There are no rocks on the property.*

He saw the lump was black, now, and, from some fifty feet away, the small boulder began to take on a definite shape. It stretched out, from the slight hump, on both sides. It, suddenly became clear to Andy this was no rock. This was a person. And, the person was very still.

Crazy Leg rushed toward his find and began licking the person's face as Trace and Andy reached the body.

Dressed in a tattered black dress, with dust turning sections of the material gray and stains spoiling its once fine needlework, was a small-framed woman with dark black hair falling below her waist.

Trace dropped to his knees in the grass and held his palm alongside the woman's cheek. She felt warm and he brushed her hair away from the dirt-stained face. She was not much more than a girl and someone, or something, had beaten her badly.

"Is she alive?" Andy asked.

"Yes, but not by much," Trace answered.

"Wonder who she is?" Andy asked.

"I don't know, but we better get her back to the house and go for help."

Trace lifted the woman into his arms.

"You bring the rifle."

"Sure," Andy answered.

In his excitement, Crazy Leg forgot the pain in his arthritic leg and jumped ahead of them showing his approval that they had come to claim his prize. He then rushed to crawl under the fence and race toward the house to announce their approach.

The young woman lay limp in Trace's arms. She had no will left to fight anymore, had she been conscious to care enough to do so. Her slight weight was an easy burden for Trace to carry.

Andy rushed for the fence to hold the wires down and let Trace lift his long legs over cautiously.

Seth was already on the porch. He was anxious to see what Crazy Leg was so excited about. He came running toward Trace and Andy.

"Who's that?"

"We don't know," Andy replied. "Apparently she's why Crazy Leg was carrying on so."

The woman stirred, slightly, in Trace's arms. He heard her moan, as he turned sideways to step over the threshold and go through the front door of the house. The two smallest children were playing with clothespin dolls on the floor with Rosie. They all looked up to see what Trace had in his arms. Rosie stood slowly, her eyes wide with disbelief. Molly, having rested and made her way back down to the living room, watched from the rocking chair near the low fire. She started to get up.

"No, Molly. Stay where you are. Rosie, lay out those pillows on the floor over there against the wall. I'll put her there until we can get Doc Landry to look at her. Andy, you head for his office and bring him back here—fast. I don't think she needs any more carting around right now."

Rosie moved to do as Trace directed. He bent to one knee and gently laid the young woman on the large cushions Molly had made for the youngsters to sit on.

Trace went to get a wet cloth to cleanse and cool the woman's face. He hoped the dampness would bring her around, at least enough to find out who she was—and why she was alongside their property.

Rosie straightened the girl's legs so that her bare feet lay with the heels against the floor. She tried to make her as comfortable as possible.

As Trace ran the cool washcloth over the woman's face, she rolled her head but still remained unconscious.

They heard Comet's hooves beat against the hard-packed ground of the drive in front of the house, and then diminish, as Andy ran him toward the main road.

Trace rose to his feet and stood looking down at the woman.

"Apparently, she's Mexican. Whether she's from around here or not, it's hard to say," he told Molly. "My guess is she's not."

"Is she a princess?" Rosie asked in awe, remembering the stories she had read in school about queens and kings and princes and princesses.

"No, I doubt that," Trace chuckled despite the young woman's dilemma, "but, she might well be from a well-to-do Mexican family. Something tells me someone, somewhere, is looking for her. How she got to us is anybody's guess."

Who are you? Why are you here? Who left you in such a deplorable condition? Was there an accident? Or, was there some coward that beat you within an inch of you life and then dumped you in such an out-of-the-way place as ours? The questions spun in his head as he waited for her to come to, or for Andy to return with Doc Landry.

Three

Several days prior to Trace and Andy finding the young woman on their property, she had been in the midst of planning a celebration at her father's *hacienda* in Mexico.

With nothing more to worry about than the color of crepe paper to hang for her brother's engagement party, Maria Carmelita Lenora Elaina Espiañata fairly danced from one task to another.

"*Madre*," she called out to her mother in another part of the house. "What do you think? Would Reyes and Trakita like this one?"

"Maria, *mia*, how can I tell? I am in the pantry with my head between the flour bin and the wall looking for the special tins I bought for preparing treats," her mother replied with only the slightest bit of irritation in her voice.

Maria shrugged and chose the brightest of the two papers she held in her hands. If it wasn't what Reyes desired, it would have to do. Besides, she was not all that happy with him for choosing Trakita to be his bride. She had hoped he would ask her best friend, Lena, but that never happened. Now, she was torn between her loyalty to Lena and her love for Reyes and it didn't seem right, to her, that Trakita would join the family instead of her best friend.

She and Lena could have had so much fun preparing for the party. Now, instead, Lena was on the sidelines and she was choosing the decorations herself. She fought the urge to pout until excitement won out and she sang a merry song as she tied bows out of the turquoise crepe paper.

From the shadows behind the *hacienda*, a serious-faced *vaquero* watched as Maria skipped in and out of the house to the verandah picking up more and more decorations to dress the rooms.

Her movements tweaked his heart and his mouth threatened to smile, but he reprimanded himself sternly and held his lips firm. He'd had a soft spot in his heart for Maria since she was fourteen and he'd first rode with her brother Reyes.

Now, banished from the *ranchero* by her brother for involving him in a plan to steal a horse for Maria, he stood in the shadows. His horse was tied behind the outbuildings where he planned that no one would see it.

Reyes would surely kill him if he found him here. He would probably shoot little chunks of flesh from his body, torturing him until he finally died. *It would not be a pleasant way to go.* But, his love for Maria was stronger than his fear of Reyes and he remained watching the brief glimpses she unknowingly offered him.

She moved, again to the verandah, and stood for a second looking in his direction.

He pulled himself further against the side of the building into the shadows and held his breath, praying she didn't see him. Yet, secretly in his mind telling himself she saw and returned his ardor.

Her long black hair glistened from a shaft of sunlight that broke through the side of the vine-covered arch of the verandah. The brightness against her long white cotton dress was almost blinding and he was struck by the contrast of the black hair and the searing white light.

He wanted to run up to her and clutch her in his arms and kiss her generous lips. He restrained himself. *I must wait. The day will come. Not now. Not now.*

Then, as quickly as Maria had appeared, she bobbed back into the big living room of the Espiañata *hacienda*.

Jesus turned and, pressing his body against the outer wall of the building that hid him, worked his way back around to his horse.

~ * ~

Two days later, near dusk, the Espiañata home was ready for company.

Wagons, buckboards and riders on individual horses arrived to partake of the huge spread set out on long wooden tables in the backyard beyond the surrounding verandah. A large carcass of beef turned on an open spit above glowing coals and the sizzling grease drew local dogs with its aroma. *Vaqueros "vamoosed"* them away

34

where they lined up to sit and drool beside the verandah wall, waiting for someone to toss them a bone. *Señoritas* shooed the flies from the food with large fronds from nearby trees.

Fiesta music filled the air as a *Mariachi* band moved amidst the jovial crowd, stopping to sing, here and there, before each small audience.

Everyone was dressed in brightly colored clothes as they danced and sang along with the music, awaiting the entrance of the guests of honor.

As darkness approached, servants lit large candles inside colored glass globes surrounding the yard.

When, at last, it was dark enough beside the outbuildings to hide him, Jesus took up his position once more. He watched the crowd, searching out Maria in her dress of multi-colored bands stitched to a tight black bodice. The flowing skirt swirled around her body like a circular rainbow as she spun to a snappy beat with a young guest.

Jesus snarled within.

The man Maria danced with was half his age. *He is too young to have any experience. He is too young to appreciate the beauty that dances before him.* He wanted to rush forward and cut in on the partners before the song ended. But, he restrained himself. *He* dare not go there!

At the proper time, Reyes and Trakita approached the loud gathering.

A cheer raised in unison from the crowd.

"A toast," Reyes' and Maria's *padre* held a glass high

in his hand and announced.

Jesus watched intently. It was a *Fiesta*. He was nearly certain Reyes would not carry his pistols to such a celebration. *But would he have hidden a small derringer in his boot?*

In the dark, alongside the building, Jesus was dressed in black. Behind him, tied at the last building from the *hacienda*, in a covered corral, were two horses. One was his, the second, for Maria. Tied to the saddle was a bundle. Inside the bundle was a long black dress with tatted black lace trim—much less conspicuous than the one Maria wore now.

The servants poured *tequila* into small glasses for the guests to toast the couple and, when they had been perfectly blessed, Maria went back inside and returned with servants in tow carrying *piñatas* and trays full of the special sweet treats her mother had overseen the cook prepare.

Reyes and Trakita accepted the well wishes with grace and, Maria thought on Reyes' part, a somewhat cool appreciation. *Do I detect trouble in paradise? Have Reyes and Trakita had a fight?* Her head whirled with the possibilities. Reyes had always said she was sensitive to other people's feelings. *Am I picking up a thought of regret from my brother? Well, I will just ask him, when I get the chance.*

"Reyes," Maria began to tug him away from his fiancée, the mayor, and the mayor's wife.

"What is it, little one?"

"Give me a moment, please?"

"Go away, little one, can't you see I'm talking to important people?" Reyes turned aside so his words were only for her.

"*Sí*! But, I must talk to you." Reyes made her so angry! Treating her like—even calling her—a child! "*Niño, Niño, Niño*," she wanted to shout after him. Perhaps even stick out her tongue. But then, that would prove him right and she was not about to do that.

"In a bit. I'll come to the verandah. Wait for me there."

Maria ducked her head in disappointment. She had to know. Was there a chance for Lena, yet? She was sure he would tell her to mind her own business. But, if she could just ask, his reaction would tell her if he were having second thoughts about marrying Trakita.

Realizing he had hurt her feelings, Reyes turned to Maria briefly.

"You look especially grown up and beautiful tonight, little sister. Be careful someone does not steal your heart as Trakita has stolen mine," he teased and winked at her.

Slowly Maria moved to the verandah.

The covered roof made its way around the adobe house attached to a low wall that had open spaces here and there for entry.

She found the music and gaiety depressing now that she realized Reyes might well marry Trakita, whether or not he truly loved her. Her father had the second largest cattle ranch in all of Mexico, second only to their own Espiañata spread. *Surely, Reyes isn't so greedy that he'd marry to merge the two ranches into the most gigantic in all Mexico?* She pulled the off-the-shoulder top of her dress back into a more comfortable position.

Jesus watched the lean, yet voluptuous, woman/child, now seventeen, as she adjusted her dress. Her curves belied the fact of the child-like innocence of her mind above the seductive body. *No wonder Reyes protects her.* Until her mind and body met with a mutual maturity, danger lurked for her in hidden encounters—and, tonight, although Reyes didn't know it, he, Jesus, was his greatest fear.

Maria walked slowly toward the front of the verandah where she could find solitude to search out the puzzle in her head. When Reyes didn't immediately arrive, she moved to where she could sit on the low wall and watch the party proceed through the open door while she waited.

Along the outer wall the dogs were now gnawing their bones, content to ignore all action going on around them.

From his hiding spot, against the dark wall of the outer structure, Jesus' heart pounded in his chest. If Reyes heard so much as a squeak, he would be on to him and Jesus knew it.

Maria was Reyes' pride as he had been nearly twelve when she was born and had played the role of big brother beyond all imagination.

Hadn't he almost killed him once for simply stealing a beautiful black horse from that homesteader's *niño* for the *señorita?* Why had has actions made Reyes so angry? Surely, in other times, Reyes would have applauded him, instead of stringing him up by his boots in a dead tree and leaving him for the *gringo* lawmen to find him.

Ah, but he had slid his feet from his boots and made his way on back to Mexico barefoot! He might not be on Reyes', or the Espiañata, payroll any longer, but his desire for Maria had not cooled.

If they would not accept him, then he would take her for his wife.

Jesus pulled a heavy wool *serape* from behind his back and crouched to move toward the verandah where Maria sat.

He looked at the dogs, satisfied that they would not stop their business with their bones, and tried to calm his breathing as he reached the adobe wall below Maria.

Quickly he stood and whipped the *serape* around her head and pulled her backwards into his arms. Then, he fled toward the horses, the kicking girl tight within his limbs.

He slipped and cursed beneath his breath.

Holding the *serape* tight against Maria's head muffled any sounds she made, losing any protests to the chatter and noise of the crowd. Each step was further from possible detection and closer to the horses.

At a safe distance, he chuckled aloud. He had caught Reyes, and all his *vaqueros*, with their guard down. He had taken one of Reyes' most prized possessions.

"Leave me hanging in a tree!" he said aloud. "I'll show you." At that moment, he didn't know which sensation he felt the strongest: his love for Maria or his taste for revenge against Reyes.

He tied the kicking, flailing bundle across the saddle.

Hoping she was getting enough air not to smother, he quickly mounted his horse and led the second one out of the Espiañata compound. Somewhere, soon, he would remove the *serape* and let Maria fill her lungs with fresh air. *It would have to be far enough away that no one would hear her scream.*

~ * ~

At last, Jesus stopped his horse and dismounted. He moved to the second horse and tugged the *serape* from around Maria's head.

As he had expected, she filled her lungs with air, as best she could laying belly down across the saddle, and opened her mouth to scream.

The sound that she could produce would not have drawn the attention of a coyote a hundred yards away.

In the dark, Maria could not make out her captor and cursed with the strongest language she could produce from her sheltered brain.

"You jackass, turn me loose. What do you think you are doing? My brother will kill you, bit by bit, for this when he catches you!"

Jesus squatted below Maria's face.

"I think Reyes will not catch up with us. The party goes on into the night and he will be far behind if he tries."

Maria spat at his face in the dark. She knew that voice. But the facial features were dim as her eyes adjusted and she tried, desperately, to make out the line of his chin, the length of his nose.

"Who are you, you—you—son-of-a-dog?" She spoke in the most mature voice she could muster.

"Ah, I am one who has worshipped you from afar, Maria."

"I know your voice."

"It is no secret I have been in love with you for a long time. Only Reyes has kept us apart, *mi* Maria."

Maria struggled against the bindings that held her to the saddle.

"Let me up!"

"I took the cover from your face and you spit at me. What do you do if I untie you?"

"I'll stay put, I promise," she lied.

"I don't think so. I think you would run the horse and I would have to chase you. We will stop in a little while and you can change your dress while it is still dark. I promise, I won't look," Jesus chuckled in a lurid tone.

She believed his lie as much as he had believed hers.

Jesus remounted his horse and started the animals across the desert toward the *Rio Grande*. Soon they would be across the border. He knew places there to hide. True, Reyes knew them, too, but there were too many for him to search them all. The chance of Reyes picking the right cave along the mountains was remote.

"I have been planning this for some time," Jesus spoke over his shoulder to Maria. "I have a camp where there are supplies. We can lay low there for a bit, then go on. Reyes will not find us, I promise you that."

"He will," Maria shrieked. "Yes, he will!"

An hour before dawn, Jesus stopped the horses in a ravine. Maria, exhausted from bouncing across the saddle all night cried out, "let me down, now!"

"*Uno momento*, my sweet," Jesus said as he moved ahead in the dark holding the reins of his horse with one hand and reaching for the limbs of a tree with the other. He grasped the branches and pulled them away from a small cave opening barely large enough for a horse to duck its head and get inside the shelter.

Jesus tugged at his horse's reins as the mount stubbornly refused to enter the cavern. Maria's horse attempted to rear but was brought down short by the tether tied to Jesus' saddle horn. Finally, Jesus managed to maneuver both animals into the cave.

Inside, the cavern opened up to the size of a small house. Jesus tied the horses to the side and began to unknot the leather thongs holding Maria's wrists.

"We'll spend the day here so you can get some rest." He lifted her down but left her feet bound. He untied the bundle with the black dress and tossed it to her. "Here, put this on while I get some light in here so you can see what you're doing."

"I won't!"

"Yes, you will. If you don't, I'll tie you back up and do it for you. Now, take off that dress and put the other one on."

He bent to light an already prepared campfire.

Maria saw the flame ignite and grow. Quickly, she did as she was told to avoid changing with the man watching her. She carefully rolled her party dress up and wrapped its bright colors with the paper that had been around the dark dress she now wore.

"You finished?"

"Yes," she said wanting to move to the growing fire and rub the chill from her arms.

The man stood up and turned her way.

"Jesus!" she said when she recognized him in the firelight. "What is the matter with you? Why are you doing this?"

"I told you. I love you. I want to marry you."

"Never!" Maria hissed back at him. "My family would never permit it," she tried futilely. "Take me back, right now, and I'll get them to let you go. They'll never hurt you, if I tell them you didn't harm me."

Jesus was close to her, now. She could feel his hot breath on the back of her neck. He lifted her hair away with his fingers and she cringed.

If she fought him, here, she felt she would lose. Her escape was blocked by the fire on one side of the cave and Jesus on the other. She stiffened as she felt his chapped lips against the back of her neck.

How long would it take for someone to miss her at the party? Surely, they were looking for her already.

"Don't," she muttered weakly, not wanting to anger Jesus and pay the consequences. "Please, let me get some rest."

Jesus moved aside as if considering his options.

"Of course. I'll get the *serape*. You can wrap up in that and get some sleep." If he didn't rush her, perhaps she would come to him willingly.

Maria shivered when he wrapped the *serape* around her shoulders. She moved away from him and curled up near the fire with her back to the wall and her face toward the cave opening. *If I get a chance*, she thought as sleep began to overcome her, *I'll slip through the cave opening while Jesus is asleep.*

Jesus wrapped a thin leather thong through the binding on her ankles and tied it to his leg.

"There," he said, "that will warn me if you try to get away while we sleep."

She yanked the *serape* more tightly around her cold shoulders.

It was a long ride between the *Rio Grande* and Jesus' destination outside Moriarty, New Mexico.

When Jesus called for Maria to mount her horse the next evening, she pulled the tail of the black dress between her legs. When she sat in the saddle the way a man rode, the full skirt formed a sort of pants leg effect giving her freedom to ride more comfortably than slung over the saddle like a loose sack of flour.

Jesus tied a rope around her waist and knotted it to the saddle horn. Then he tied the lead rope to his saddle horn.

"What's this?" He lifted the brown-paper wrapped package.

"My *Fiesta* dress. Surely you don't expect me to wear

this horrid thing forever?"

Reluctantly, he tied the bundle in front of her, attaching it, too, to the saddle horn.

As they rode, Maria managed to rip a small hole in the paper until the very edge of her dress's bright colors stuck out from the wrapping. She worked the threads in the hem apart and pulled small strips of the fabric away, dropping them behind her as they rode.

It isn't much, but Reyes will know—she knew he would.

"By now, they're looking for me, you know," she called to Jesus' back as they edged their way up a canyon.

Jesus ignored her.

"Reyes will never stop hunting you!"

"*Callarse!* Be silent or I'm going to make you take the lead. I will let you be the one to get switched in the face with branches and see how you like it." He jerked on the lead rope in an attempt to quiet her.

She fell silent and he smugly told himself he had won that battle. She had fire and he liked that in a woman. But, he would not be controlled by one. She would submit to him, one way or the other. The choice was hers, whether it would be difficult or easy, but she would submit.

Four

Travel for Jesus and Maria progressed slowly. Maria continued to do what she could to slow their pace while Jesus countered her efforts. He wished to get to flat country so they could pick up their speed.

"Where are we going?" Maria asked plaintively at one point.

"Don't worry about it. I have a plan," Jesus told her.

Outside of Estancia, New Mexico, Jesus had signed on with a cattle outfit, then arranged to take the time to return to Mexico and pick up "his wife" who he promised would cook for the ranch hands.

The scrawny, aging bunkhouse cook had dismissed Jesus' boasts as unbelievable. Jesus could still see the scorn in the man's eyes. He would show him. Not only would Maria cook, she would be the most beautiful thing the men had ever seen.

He jerked the lead rope to encourage Maria's horse to keep up.

Maria was tired, dirty and growing more angry with each passing hour. *Why hasn't Reyes caught up with us by now?* She had been leaving her colorful trail behind until very little was left of her *fiesta* dress and she had to hide twigs in the wrapper to make the paper seem still full of the fabric.

They had seen no one on the trails they had taken. The route was chosen by Jesus for precisely that reason. She felt physically sick and definitely homesick. Hot tears threatened behind her eyes, but she would not give Jesus the satisfaction of seeing her cry.

"Just wait until you get to your new home," Jesus said. "You're going to like it there."

"I want to go back to my own home, you mule. Turn me loose. Let me find my own way!"

"No, *señorita,* we cannot turn back now. We are so close."

Ahead, Jesus could see that the sky was black. They were coming out of the mountains into a low-lying area and he didn't like the looks of the clouds hanging overhead. He listened intently for the far-off rumble of thunder. It was still dry where they were, but a sudden storm in the mountains could send the water rushing down the stream beds.

"*Prisa!* We must go *pronto.*"

Maria resisted, hoping to slow her horse with signals she gave by leaning her body further back on the saddle and pressing her feet forward in the stirrups.

"No, Maria, for your own safety, we must go now."

She sensed Jesus' concern. Still, she tried to slow the horse.

"We are between two streams here," Jesus pointed out the fork of the rocky dry creek beds on either side of them. "If the water comes, we will be washed away.

Come, we must hurry."

"Hurry, yourself. Leave me behind!"

"Have you not seen a flash flood before? The water will come through here so fast we will not be able to escape!"

Maria could tell Jesus was nearing panic, now. She felt a slight chill of fear run down her spine. Could they be swept away by a sudden rush of water here? It seemed so peaceful. There was no sign of rain where they were. She looked to the sky and studied the clouds in the distance. She remembered her brother, Reyes, had warned her of storms and what to look for if she was caught out in the desert and a thunderstorm was approaching.

Perhaps I better do as he says.

As she urged her horse to a quicker pace, she heard a horrendous roar like she had never known before.

"Come!" Jesus shouted above the noise. He headed for the high side of the dry creek bottom away from the mountains they had come through earlier that day.

Before his horse could climb the bank to safety, she saw the churning water fast approaching. It was like froth on top of weak chocolate where the silt and water boiled together. Then, it hit them. Maria felt the full force of the wall of water sweep over her from behind as she kicked her horse to run for the bank. The wave swept her horse off its feet and whisked her, still astride the saddle, along with him. Her hands were free, but her waist was still tied to the saddle. All she could do was tumble with the animal as the swirling water churned mud and liquid, agitating them with limbs and branches, roiling the sandy creek bottom in its foam.

Jesus, still clinging to the lead rope was washed from his mount and tried to swim through the chaos toward Maria.

His horse, having been knocked to its haunches, had recovered and climbed to the top of the bank.

Maria tried to catch breaths of air while she worked to free herself from the bindings that kept her on the struggling horse.

The water tightened the knots even more and she felt her fingers burn as she tried to undo the thongs.

"Hang on!" Jesus called as he grasped the fingers of his right hand in the horse's mane and reached his other arm back toward her. Maria saw the flash of a knife blade in the brief moment she was above water. Then she saw Jesus lose his grip and the water rushed his lighter weight over the horse and past them. He sank under water and she didn't see him again.

In the next moment, she realized her horse was moving away from her. She was no longer tied to the saddle.

A small tree limb punched her in the ribs, then floated past her. Still another and another hit her until she could no longer catch her breath. She felt herself tumbling beneath the surface. There was nothing left but blackness and the limp girl was carried downstream until the water ran its course, then threw her aside as it diminished in a fan of wetness across the desert floor. It soaked into the ground at the end of the left fork of the creek as quickly as it had come.

Maria lay on the creek bank throughout the night and into the next day. In the heat of the day, curious vultures flew by, but refused to land when the breeze flapped the hem of her black dress in their direction. At last, a small group of birds settled in the sagebrush around her and watched patiently.

Near the end of the day, the breeze died down as the daylight dimmed. The birds dropped to the ground, forming a circle around the black-covered thing before them.

They set up a squawking argument over who should start feasting where, raising a din so loud it was sure to attract the attention of any passerby.

The bravest bird moved toward Maria.

Slowly, very slowly, she moved one finger, then another. The motion took all the energy she had. She blacked out again.

But, it had been enough to send the scouting bird skittered back, erupting all of the birds into a screeching commotion.

Gradually, Maria was able to move her legs and finally pushed herself a few inches off the creek bank with her arms. She turned her head and stared at the ugly, foul-smelling birds.

"Go away," her coarse voice whispered. She collapsed to rest and muster enough strength to try again.

The carrions, discouraged that their meal would not be served, scattered back to the bushes to watch and await the possibility that there may still be a feast.

Finally, inch-by-inch, Maria managed to pull herself across the sand to the rough cut bank. There she again collapsed. She leaned her back against this newest obstacle while she rested to try to climb atop onto what she hoped would be solid ground above the waterway.

As she sat regaining her strength, she looked about her. She saw no sign of Jesus or either of the horses. If any of them had survived, they weren't where she could tell.

If Jesus hadn't saved her life by cutting her free, she would think it served him right if he had drown, she thought before surrendering herself to another lapse of unconsciousness.

When she awoke, again, the buzzards were near her feet staring longingly at her. She picked up small pebbles and weakly tossed them in their direction scattering them, once and for all, she hoped. She slept through the night and then, with daylight, managed to climb over the bank and, unable to stand, drag her body along in a direction away from the creek bed that now held only a trickle of water. Her ribs were sore from the battering her body had taken in the water and there were bruises all over her that ached. She knew she had to keep going.

As she lay on her belly to rest in the grit, she looked about and found that the land was basically flat for miles and miles ahead. There were no signs of buildings, or hills, or trees. There was nothing but prairie as far as she could tell. She was resigned to keep going as long as she could and as far as she could. *Perhaps someone will wander along and find me.* She laid her ear to the ground, hoping to hear the sound of hoof beats. She heard nothing.

Gradually, she pulled herself along until she could, at last, crawl.

Finally, she saw a break in the distant horizon.

It was a fence. *If there is a fence, there must be people that check the fence.*

When she reached the fence, she saw the roofline of a

house, and the pitch of others on outbuildings, ahead. She passed out again before she could reach them.

~ * ~

"Child! Child!" Maria heard someone calling. It made her angry. *Who is calling me a niño?* Her mind was groggy. She hated it when Reyes called her that.

She fought the blackness of unconsciousness.

Is it Reyes? No, no. He would call me 'little one.' Not a 'niño' knowing how angry it makes me.

Slowly she moved her head and moaned at the pain she felt when she did.

Voices fluctuated in and out of her ears.

She tried to open her eyes, but the lids did not want to cooperate. Her lashes were too heavy to lift and she saw only through small slits.

"Don't worry, child, the swelling will go down soon. Just rest," the man's voice spoke soothingly.

"Maria," she muttered.

It was a whisper.

"Maria," the voice repeated.

"Well, Maria, I am going to fix you some medicine. You'll be fit as a fiddle before you even know it," the unfamiliar voice of Doc Landry encouraged.

Maria dozed again.

When she awoke she was in a bed in a bright room.

Her eyelids were no longer too swollen to uncover her eyes.

"Trace," a woman called out. "Trace, she's awake."

The woman moved to the door, then came back.

"How are you feeling, Maria?"

"Better," Maria answered hearing her voice echo in the

room.

"Good. We've been spoon feeding you broth and doing everything we could think of to help you get your health back. My name's Molly Westerman. You certainly had us worried."

"Molly? Thank you for helping me."

A large man rushed in through the door. He grinned from ear to ear. "Say, you sure had us scared there for awhile."

"You rest now," Molly said.

"You're safe here. We'll take care of you," the man said. "When you're ready to talk, you can tell us what happened."

What happened? What happened? Maria began to put the pieces together in her mind, tiring too soon to finish the job.

~ * ~

The next morning, Maria was awake shortly after dawn. The aroma of food cooking wafted to her from the room below.

"Good Morning, sleepyhead," her host, Trace Westerman greeted her from where he stood in the doorway with a tray of food in his hands.

Maria pushed herself up, resting her shoulders on the large pillows. Molly, already in the room ahead of Trace, moved to situate the pillows better.

"How are you feeling, today?" Molly asked.

"Much better."

Trace smiled at her as he sat the tray beside her.

"We thought your appetite might be up to something substantial this morning," Trace told her.

She looked at the plate. Her stomach growled with hunger as she saw scrambled eggs, side pork and preserved apple slices before her. A tin cup of milk sat next to the food.

"It looks good."

"Thank you," Molly said. "We put up the apples before I got sick."

Molly turned away, toward the window, remembering her own close call with death.

Trace gave her a moment, then moved a chair beside her over to the bed and motioned for her to sit down. He straddled the seat of another chair to sit so his arms rested on the back and lowered his chin to his forearms.

"Molly had some sort of heart attack late last summer."

"That is terrible," Maria said, her voice, used to speaking Spanish, drawing the words out awkwardly and, still, weakly.

"Tell us about yourself," Trace invited more brightly. "We know your name is Maria. We don't know how you got here or how you got so beaten up."

Maria looked at her arms. The bruises were faint marks now.

"I—I got caught in a flash flood. I guess the things I was thrown against and the limbs that hit me must have caused the bruises." She let out a long string of Spanish words in frustration at trying to explain competently in English.

Trace's mind labored to catch the words and interpret them. He shook his head with puzzlement.

He recognized a couple of swear words and a man's name.

"Who is Jesus?" He asked.

"Jesus—he worked on our *rancho*, in Mexico, for my brother and my *padre*. He took me away from my home and wouldn't let me go back."

Trace rose to his feet in shock.

"Where is he now?"

"I don't know. Perhaps he was killed in the flood."

"But you aren't sure?"

"No. I am grateful to be away from him—to be alive. My family will pay you *mucho dinero* for saving me."

"That's not necessary," Molly told her as she reached out to pat her hand. "Here, we do what we can for our neighbors. Please, have your breakfast and rest some more. Soon, we will sort all this out. Would you like me to stay with you?"

Molly straightened the brightly colored patchwork quilt along its edges as she waited, patiently, for Maria to answer.

A wail came from the kitchen.

"Did, too," Seth's voice carried up the stairs.

"No—no," Emmy's baby talk came back.

Maria looked at Molly.

"I think you are needed elsewhere, no?"

Molly laughed. "You'll meet the rest of the family later. "We won't let the little ones climb the stairs. The children all saw you when you were brought in. They are all very curious about you."

Maria looked questioningly at Trace.

"We left you downstairs until Doc Landry took a good look at you and said we could move you up here."

Molly got up and moved to the door. She turned toward

the stairs. She was concerned at leaving Maria, but drawn to the urgency below.

"I have to go help Rosie with the babies. You let me know if you need anything," she said.

"Thank you."

"Later, we'll talk about finding your family," Trace said as he raised himself from the chair where he had sat back down. He followed Molly.

When she was alone Maria took a small bite of the scrambled eggs and savored it on her tongue. Her mouth wasn't back to normal yet and the size of her tongue surprised her. Had she come so close to death she had seen The Madonna? Or was it only the blurred vision of the woman that had helped her? Whichever, she prayed she never had to go through an experience like that again.

Surely, she had suffered enough.

But, somewhere between the Westerman homestead and Mexico, someone else thought differently.

Five

Jesus, having managed to escape the turbulent water rushing him down stream, had lain on the bank several hundred feet away from where he had last seen Maria. He was less battle-weary than Maria and less beaten. His horse was gone, having lost its footing on the crumbling bank and fallen into the roiling water again. It had been washed past him heading south, toward Mexico, should it survive.

Maria was uppermost in Jesus' mind. *What if Maria isn't dead? What if she had managed to escape and headed back to Mexico and her family?* He was a dead man, if she reached the Espiañata *rancho* and reported what had transpired. If Reyes caught him, he would be a goner. His euphoria at having survived the flash flood faded as he sat, letting water and grit drain from every part of his body and clothing. He dug packed sand from his ears and snorted it from his nose while he assessed his possible fate.

With what little might he had left, he pulled himself, dripping wet, across the ground until he could find a bush tough enough with which to drag his sagging body upright. Then, he picked up a branch and used it as a crutch to help drag his sore and aching frame along the ground.

A rattlesnake buzzed a warning nearby.

Adrenaline reserves exhausted, along with his body, Jesus slowly swung the branch he used as a crutch in the direction of the sound and crunched the snake's head beneath the sand before falling, once again, into the dirt.

Damn snake, he thought when the fear subsided. He looked about wondering if the snake had traveled with a partner and moved cautiously as he righted himself again.

He walked the edge of the creek's bank, upstream, until he reached the area where he and Maria had been caught in the tumbling water.

"Maria," he called out to no avail. Either she was dead or not within the sound of his voice, or she would not answer preferring to die than have him find her.

And, who could blame her? He experienced a brief lucid moment. The deed he had done, and its results, turned like a lump in his stomach and even he felt a slight—very slight—revulsion for his actions.

How could he have caused the death of one so beautiful? Someone so *mucho* desirable? Another *gringo*? Another enemy? He wouldn't think twice before drawing his gun or running them through with his knife. But, Maria! Maria was to be his whole life—his whole world, whether she liked it or not.

Now, he could only stumble on in a daze wondering where her body would be found or if it ever would be.

If Reyes was the one to find her, he would not stop tracking him until he captured him and cut tiny sections from his hide. The possibility made him step more lively and he pushed on, hoping to find, or steal, a horse at the next homestead. He would not rest easy until he was sure he could stay way ahead of Reyes Espiañata. He knew, whether Maria was found or not, he would be looking over his shoulder for the rest of his life.

~ * ~

At the Kling/Westerman homestead, Maria was getting stronger with each passing day. She insisted, now, on being up as much as her aching body would allow. She had not ventured out of the bedroom yet. Her hosts, eager to have her do so, encouraged her to leave the room and, while they waited for her to gather her courage and go downstairs with them, they anxiously quizzed her about her home and family. They looked for clues to return her, safely, to those that loved her.

Now that her mind was clear her English was quite understandable and she explained to Trace and Molly as they sat talking, "My father saw to it that all of the people in his household spoke your language."

"Your family must be terribly worried about you," Molly said solemnly, thinking about the times in the past when something frightening had happened to someone in her own family. She well remembered the time Rosie was thrown from the buckboard and almost died. When she regained consciousness, she had the uncanny ability to foretell future events. She had lost that gift, now, and Molly thought, perhaps, that would have been a help in solving the question about Maria's roots. Doc Landry had said Maria might have a slight amnesia—a memory loss. He hoped it would be temporary, if that were the case.

Molly thought how ironic it was, that there were things Maria either couldn't, or wouldn't, remember and Rosie had been so alert to things she couldn't have possibly known. *The mind is a very curious thing.*

"Yes, I am sure they are," Maria agreed. "Normally, I travel with a chaperone, my lovely *tia* Consuelo," she said remembering pleasanter trips. "This Jesus! He is a thief! A murderer!"

"Other than your kidnapping, do you have any proof that he has killed someone?" Trace hoped they might be able to give the sheriff more information and get him involved in a man hunt, if her statement was true.

"No."

"If we could prove any of this—" Trace contemplated.

"You said your father saw to it that you could speak our language—" Molly encouraged Maria to go on in hopes that the thoughts would spur her mind back to normalcy.

A strange look flickered across Maria's brown eyes. She hesitated to continue her earlier conversation.

"*Si!* Yes. My *Padre* was very young, perhaps even younger than your Andy, when he was sent to carry ammunition for the *compatriots* at the battle at the adobe your people now call The Alamo. He saw the destruction. The death. He vowed, after the Americans were killed at the little mission, that, should he have a family, they would all be taught how to understand the confusing American words. He wanted no "accident" befalling his family because they didn't understand their neighbors."

Trace nodded.

He observed her abrupt change of demeanor.

Rosie, having settled the babies down for a nap, entered the room and sat on the floor next to Molly as the group talked. She shuddered as if a chill ran down her spine.

"Perhaps you might like to go out into the sunshine?" Trace suggested to Maria when he noticed Rosie shake slightly from the chill.

"Yes. That would be very nice, sometime."

"But she must not go beyond the windmill," Rosie cautioned.

Had Rosie's sudden tremor been a sign that she sensed something no one else knew? Trace wondered. She'd had premonitions when she was a couple of years younger. They had started right after the wagon accident that had put her into a coma. When she awoke for the first time, it was with a vision of Andy being thrown from Comet during a lightning storm. But, Trace thought that was all behind them, now. Rosie hadn't "seen" anything for some time.

Both Molly and Trace looked at Rosie with questioning eyes.

"It's just—she'd probably feel safer staying close to the house," Rosie explained remembering how uncertain she had felt after her own accident.

Another thought occurred to Trace, *Maria has yet to tell us her last name.*

It was becoming clear to Molly, by Maria's hesitation, that she was not about to go downstairs without more encouragement.

"Rosie, would you go down and make some tea?" Molly rose slowly and moved toward the door. "I think it is time Maria joins the rest of the family."

"Use the china teapot," she added as Rosie squeezed past her in the doorway. Maria was a guest and she wanted her treated as such. Perhaps she had finer things in her home and using the china might be a small way to help bring back her memory.

When Rosie reached the kitchen, she filled a teakettle with water and set it on the stove to heat. Trace had found a location to buy coal by the gunnysack and they burned that in the cook stove, now, both for heat and for cooking. It put off an acrid odor and created a fine black dust that had to be cleaned from the house constantly, but the heat was consistent and the chunks remained coals far longer than what wood they could manage to bring in from the mountain.

Ever since the trauma of Molly's attack, Rosie had fought the urge to crawl behind the stove, between the heat and the wall, and curl up like a kitten. She watched Callie, her Calico cat, lying there now, as she stretched and adjusted her body to the radiating heat that intensified with Rosie's stoking of the fire.

She'd like to join Callie, there, in the serenity of her sanctuary.

These urges had been coming on her more frequently, and she wondered why. Sometimes, she felt like a kitten instead of a human being. So far, she had resisted carrying out the ideas that flirted with her mind. She thought she would feel safe there behind the radiating heat of the stove. She thought she would feel warm and secure and free from all the cares of the world.

It still concerned her to think how close they came to

losing Molly. She worried that the horrible attack might happen again. She couldn't put the thought of Molly dying out of her head. She felt so small, so afraid. It was a big world out there and, without Molly, Rosie wasn't sure she could survive on her own.

Occasionally, when she awoke some mornings, she found she had curled into a ball in the midst of her covers and her arm was wet where she had licked it. Why was she doing, or wanting to do, these strange things?

She heard Trace and Molly helping Maria toward a chair behind her. Their conversation jogged her mind away from the strange feelings.

She turned, relieved that their presence gave her determination to break away from her thoughts. She lifted the kettle and moved it to a hotter position on the stovetop.

"Careful, now," Trace was saying as Maria moved on still unsteady legs. Trace pulled a kitchen chair out from the table for her to sit down. He scooted another away from the table for Molly. Then, spun a third around and straddled it backwards, resting his arms across the rounded back that the spindles supported.

"Tell us more about your family, Maria. Perhaps I can do something to get you back home."

Molly nodded. "Trace is familiar with the Texas border area."

Maria studied this strong, gentle man across from her. *I have never known a gringo before that was so handsome and kind.* All she had known were old *Padres* that came, sometimes, to Mexico to teach their religion. She had never thought that there might be younger, stronger, more fascinating men across the border. *Molly is very fortunate to have such a good husband.* Maria felt a touch of envy squeeze her heart. Why must she be always pursued by the likes of Jesus? Because her *Padre* was wealthy and owned hundreds of acres of land, every *vaquero* in Mexico seemed to vie for her attention. She was tired of that. She was bored! She wanted to find someone who would love her for herself—not for her father's riches!

Sheltered by her family, she had been allowed only light flirtations with fine Mexican gentlemen while they held the *vaqueros* at bay. Although her father had not broached the subject yet, she was certain he had already arranged a marriage for her with one of the most eligible men in all of Mexico.

This, she did not want. She wanted to find her own young man, and fall in love, and run away, if necessary, to be happy. An arranged marriage was not for her.

Andy came into the kitchen with Seth and Emmy tagging along behind him.

"I found these two playing in the mud at the water trough," he told Molly.

Molly laughed and grasped Emmy's hands, holding her at arm's length. She was far muddier than Seth.

"You certainly need a bath. I thought sure you were napping."

"She woke up and we went out to play," Seth defended their actions.

"Seth, go wash up."

"Yes, Ma." Seth went toward the door to return to the trough and clean the dirt from his hands and face.

"And get some clean pants," Molly added.

Maria smiled at Andy. He seemed to have the kindness and gentle actions similar to what Trace demonstrated. Perhaps he had learned them at the older man's side. *He will be a fine man, himself, someday.*

Trace, mistaking her reverie as the possibility she were tiring, asked, "Do you want to go back upstairs and lie down?"

"No," Maria answered quietly, "I am fine. I was only thinking." Perhaps, in the end, Jesus might have done her a favor. His taking her away from her family might well have provided her the opportunity to look for romance with someone different than her father's choosing. She was stronger now. Her family, although surely worried, had not come looking for her. Perhaps Reyes needed a lesson. He was always bossing her around. Perhaps it would be her turn to show him she could run her own life her own way.

She might find someone to take a message to her mother to let her know she was alive and well, beyond that, why should she rush back to Mexico?

Perhaps, if she didn't get well too quickly, she could get to know Andy better, perhaps look this strange world over from a better point of view.

Rosie set a steaming cup of tea in front of Maria and brought a sugar bowl, which nearly matched the cup and teapot, and a spoon to the table. She poured another cup of the hot liquid for Molly and set it near the dishpan where Molly had set the stripped Emmy in a pan of warm soapy water on the kitchen counter.

Callie came out from behind the stove and rubbed her body against Rosie's bare foot. The cat's fur was hot against her skin and she reached down and picked her up. She felt the soft underbelly of the cat and her fingers bumped its ribcage. Callie was relaxed within Rosie's grasp and all four of her legs drooped as Rosie wrapped her arm around the cat's belly. Callie's body adjusted to Rosie's grip, her form fitting perfectly within the wrap of Rosie's arms. Callie rubbed her chin across Rosie's left arm, her lips tightening against her teeth until Rosie felt their needlelike nudge on her arm. Callie purred.

Rosie edged her way back to the china teapot and, as if sensing her next move, Trace spoke.

"None for me, thanks. Andy and I have chores to do. Andy, we need to mend fence on the back line before the cattle get out. Have you fed the chickens yet, Rosie?"

Rosie dropped Callie onto the crocheted rug in front of the fireplace.

"I'll do it as soon as I finish my tea. Maria, can I help you get settled somewhere first?"

"I'll be fine here," Maria assured her as she sipped her first taste of sweet sassafras tea. When she tipped her cup, she looked up at Andy through her long, dark lashes.

"This is wonderful, Rosie," she said as she smelled the pungent aroma and tasted the flavor of the liquid on her tongue.

Molly turned back toward the girls as she held Emmy firmly, by her soap-slick skin, in the warm water.

"I know it's a bit early for sassafras, but we've run out of black tea. Besides, a little blood thinning probably won't hurt any of us," Molly told the girls.

Trace rose and left the house with Andy, leaving the two girls watching Jacob play on the floor while Molly cuddled Emmy in a small blanket to dry.

Maria continued to sip her hot tea slowly as she ran pleasant thoughts through her mind. She felt a little rush of excitement in her heart. Andy was definitely someone she could become very enamored with. But, she was becoming too tired to even entertain thoughts, now, beyond her own recovery.

Molly noticed Maria's stature sag. She noted that Callie had wandered over to the pillows stacked in the corner of the living room and climbed to the top. She lay, now, curled on top of the pile.

"Rosie, why don't you move Callie off the pillows? Please lay them out flat on the floor for Maria to rest on."

"You have been so kind, Molly. Your whole family has been wonderful. How can I ever thank you?"

"There's no need to. That's what neighbors are for. When you feel like talking more, maybe you can tell us something that will help us find your family so you can go home when you are ready. Perhaps even your last name will help."

"But, they are so far away," Maria said sadly. She was not ready to give up any further information. She would fake a dulled memory and use her exhaustion to her own benefit.

"I will rest now."

~ * ~

Outside, Andy rode Comet to the barn and dropped to the ground before tugging the reins over the horse's head and letting the leather straps hang loose. He knew the horse wouldn't go anywhere as long as the straps hung there, whether he tied them to a rail or not. It had been his experience that the only way the horse would leave was if someone led him away and that wasn't likely to happen the few minutes he spent in the barn helping Trace gather fencing tools.

Trace saddled Lucky for the ride to the back fence line and Andy asked about Maria.

"How much longer do you think Maria will stay?"

"She's pretty isn't she?" Trace asked assessing Andy's interest in her. "She's doing better. In a few weeks she should be well enough to travel back to Mexico."

"I guess someone could call her that, if they like dark black hair and eyes that seem to hide secrets, then flash when she doesn't like something someone says," Andy replied with more maturity than Trace expected.

Ah, Andy has thought this girl through. Already he was beginning to register women in his young brain for their attributes as well as their offenses. Trace had seen Molly's tenaciousness as stubbornness, at first, until he understood that her unwillingness to give up was what had kept the family together. And, damn any man who tried to break it up! He had learned, early on, that Molly put family first and she wasn't about to let that change. He admired her for that. The solution, for him, was to fall in love with Molly and marry her. So, now, he, too, was part of her family. Andy should be so fortunate as to find a woman as kind, generous and good hearted as Molly was when he reached an age to marry.

Trace studied Andy as he stood fidgeting with a long shaft of hay.

"Is something wrong, Andy?"

"No. It's good that she'll soon go back to her own

family." Andy was uneasy about having this pretty young woman in the house and he couldn't explain why. She was beautiful and, no doubt, would raise the eyebrow of any cowboy or farmhand that had the opportunity to meet her. Not that he was interested. Visions of Becky took up most of the time he had for idle thoughts. When he could, he slipped away to see her without filling Trace in on his whereabouts.

Trace noted the less than fully welcome tone in Andy's voice.

"Why are you in a rush to have her leave?"

"I'm not. It's just that—I'm sure her family is worried about her," Andy answered, blushing with shame at his apparent lack of compassion. "It's just, well, I told Becky about us finding her. She didn't like it, very much, that she was staying here. She thought we should go to the sheriff and let him look for her relatives."

"When we feel she's well enough to travel, I will," Trace assured him.

Andy nodded.

"Until then, she's welcome in our home and I don't want any more argument about it—from you or Becky. Understand?"

"Yes, sir."

"People have helped us when we've needed it," he reminded Andy. "I'd suggest, if Becky's eyes are getting too green, you let her know Maria's no threat to how you feel about her."

"Yes, sir. I'll do that." Andy answered feeling relieved that he hadn't been the only one to think Becky was showing a little jealousy. In a way, it made him feel proud to think that Becky would worry that someone else might be attracted to him. At times, he felt like the man he was becoming. At other times, he still felt like a gangly little boy with rough features out of proportion to the size of his face. Becky's concern, that there might be another girl on the horizon, made him feel strong, powerful and desirable. It made him feel like a man.

"Shucks," he added to Trace, "Maria's probably a few years older than me. Anyways, Becky's got nothing to worry about."

"Good. Now, let's get on with the fence repair." Trace was relieved to know Andy hadn't let himself be too enamored with Maria's beauty. He didn't need an even more lovesick boy in the house. It was bad enough, that Andy mooned over Becky, slipping off to see her when he thought he wasn't looking. How was he going to keep the boy from letting his heart get him in trouble if two girls showed an interest in him?

Six

The days slipped away without incident. Andy and Trace continued to maintain the homestead while Molly, with Rosie's help, preserved food, built up their stock of lye soap, watched the babies and saw to it that Maria regained her vitality. Times were good with their diet consisting now of a variety of foods due to the milk cow they had bought and small herd of beef cattle that Trace had provided.

Molly continued to allow the chickens to set, whenever possible, hatching chicks to keep the family in eggs and meat. The addition of pigs, that were allowed to run the outer perimeter of the fence line, supplied meat, including bacon, when Trace kept the smokehouse going to cure hams and slabs of meat to slice for breakfast. Molly rendered lard from the fat and used it for cooking and making soap. The pigs' other vital job was to eradicate rattlesnakes, or at least give Molly the peace of mind that they would keep them off the immediate area surrounding the house and away from the babies.

Still, there were always chores to keep Andy busy. Maria was becoming bored with her confinement and she suggested she take over milking the cow.

"You are our guest," Molly said. "You should relax and rest until you are completely well."

"But, I need to do something. It is not good that I sit all day while the rest of you work and see that I am fed. I think it is time I should help, maybe, with the cooking. Even though we had servants in my parent's home, my mother always enjoyed preparing the food as well. She taught me to make several dishes. Let me show you how to make tortillas. You can teach me how to make your stew or roast the meat."

"Andy, you can teach me to milk the cow. I am no longer too weak," Maria pleaded.

Andy looked over at Molly, questioning whether she thought Maria was strong enough to take on duties.

"Maria could be a big help," Molly said. "Milking the cow would not be too hard. That would give you more time to help Trace with the other chores." Molly assessed the nature of the milk cow she had bought from Mrs. Johnson so the family no longer needed to trek to her homestead for fresh milk. Spot and Missy, the two cows Trace had brought back from the ranch he had owned in Texas, before he came to New Mexico, were from beef stock. Their milk production was too low to supply the family's needs for dairy products. They were being used to grow the herd of beef cattle to stock the homestead.

They were too wild to even consider milking. Bossy was a gentle Jersey cow. She was small, but with a bag that held enough milk to feed the family and give the extra milk to a weaner calf that had been taken from its mother. She was sure Bossy would not be bothered by a stranger learning to milk.

"Please, I must do something!" Maria persisted.

"I will take you to the barn this evening when it is time to milk. Your hands are not as big as mine. It may not be easy."

Maria held her hands up with her fingers outstretched.

"See. They may be little but my fingers are strong now and long enough to play the guitar at my home. I am willing to learn. Teach me."

Not only could she help with the chores, it would give her some time alone with Andy. Maria let her mind play with the idea.

The teats on Bossy's udder were difficult for Andy's larger hands to grasp.

Perhaps Maria's smaller fingers would be better. Andy considered the fact that, as he grew older, his hands became larger and he had, already, begun to entertain the idea of teaching Seth to milk before the job became too difficult. He had other chores that he could put his time to right now.

"Tonight, I'll take you to the barn with me. I have to go meet up with Trace, now, and help check the fence." It was their practice to start at opposite ends of the fence line and ride until they met in the middle. That way, they reasoned, they could cover the whole fence in a shorter time, and be back in time to clean up for dinner, and to do the evening chores.

"Seth collects the eggs in the chicken house in the mornings. Maybe you can go hold the basket for him," Molly told Maria.

Maria nodded. "Of course, I will be happy to."

~ * ~

When Andy and Trace returned, Andy took the milk bucket from where it sat, upside down, on a clean flour sack. He let the bail slide through his fingers and the heavier metal bucket flip upright. He would take care of the cow before dinner.

Maria watched as he prepared to leave for the barn.

"We'll see how strong your fingers are, Maria. You can come with me."

Maria borrowed a shawl from the peg beside the door and wrapped it around her shoulders, then followed Andy outside.

They approached the barn and Andy hesitated near the entrance to scoop grain from a wooden bin to dump into the feed box.

"Bossy comes into the stanchion easier if you make sure the grain is already waiting. If you get good at this, it can be your job after while."

Maria nodded.

Andy dumped most of the grain onto the bottom of the feedbox. Then, he took the near-empty can and rattled it at the back door of the barn to entice the cow inside.

Once he had her tied in the stanchion, he sought out the three-legged milk stool Trace had built for him to sit on. He set it on the floor beside the cow and took a damp cloth he had brought to wash her bag down.

"You need to be sure to clean her good before you start to milk." Andy wrapped his fingers around two teats and began to tug. Milk spurted into the bottom of the bucket with a "zing".

"It seems easy."

"It is harder than it appears. Here, you try."

Andy stood up and gave the stool to Maria.

"Like this?" Maria asked as she wrapped her fingers around the cow's teats. She squeezed. Nothing happened.

"Kind of tug," Andy offered.

Maria tried again.

Still nothing.

The milk did not "zing" into the bucket like it had for Andy.

She tried again.

The cow swung her head back and looked through the bars of the stanchion at her.

"Careful. She might kick," Andy warned.

They were concentrating on the job at hand and did not hear a horse ride up to the house.

"Becky. What a pleasant surprise," Molly greeted the girl at the front door.

"My mother sent you some fresh greens," Becky said, handing a plump flour sack to Molly. She took a small brown bag from her skirt pocket and handed it to Seth.

"Here's some hard candy for you to share with the other kids."

"Thank you, Becky." Seth remembered his manners and his desire to be on her good side so she would bring more another time.

"After dinner, Seth." Molly reminded him. "And don't let the babies have any big pieces. Break it up for them."

"Yes, Ma." He said, disappointment showing on his face.

"Dinner is soon. You can wait."

"Andy is milking," Rosie told Becky.

"Will you stay and eat with us?" Molly offered. "It's a long ride back and you might as well join us."

"Thank you. But, I have to be home before dark. Mother said she'd save a plate of food for me."

"Go on out to the barn, if you like. I'm sure Andy will be happy to see you." Molly turned to put the greens in a pan of water. "And, be sure to tell your mother 'thank you' for me."

Becky stepped outside and headed for the gaping hole where the barn door was normally closed.

She could hear voices inside.

"Here, let me show you how," Andy said as he moved toward Maria and put his arms around her to take her hands in his and teach her how to stroke the milk from Bossy's udder.

Becky gasped as she stopped beside them.

Andy looked up when he heard the sound.

"Becky!"

Maria looked up, too, and gazed into the girl's pale blue eyes that were staring accusingly at her.

"I was showing Maria how to milk."

Becky regained her composure.

"So I saw."

Andy stood up and stepped away from Maria. He moved toward Becky.

I knew Maria's staying here was going to cause me trouble! Andy tried to think of a way to make Becky see that he was not interested in taking up with Maria.

Becky turned on her heel and started for the barn door. Trying to catch up, Andy stumbled over a board at the corner of the stall and sprawled across the floor behind her.

"Wait, Becky!"

But Becky was running now, heading for her horse. Tears stung her eyes and her heart ached.

"Andy," Maria called after him as she tugged at the cow.

Andy righted himself just as he heard the "twang" of Bossy's hoof connect with the metal pail. The sound of milk splashing through the air and splattering everywhere followed.

"Oh! *Madre Mia!*" Maria called out. "You stubborn cow! Now look what you have done!" Maria wore the milk across Molly's shawl and the white fluid dripped down her dress. She stood shaking the liquid from her hands as she looked after Andy where he followed Becky.

"Becky! Wait!" Andy called again.

He reached her as she tugged the horse's reins from the hitching rail and swung herself into the saddle.

"Becky. I was just showing her how to—"

Becky pulled the reins to the side to turn the horse away from the house. Andy reached for the saddle horn, catching the reins in his fingers as he did.

"Stop, Andy. Let me go!"

"Not until you listen to me."

Becky yanked the reins from Andy's hands and bumped her heels into the horse's sides. Andy stepped back to avoid being knocked down by the animal's rump.

"Becky!" He shouted after her in frustration.

Molly came to the door. "What's all the commotion, Andy?"

Andy stubbed his toe into the dirt, studying the dust

that surfaced. "Becky's mad because she walked up when I was showing Maria how to milk. I think she got the wrong idea about what was going on."

Maria came up to the porch with the empty milk pail in her hand. Her hair dripped milk from its dark tresses. Molly looked from Andy to Maria. She felt a tug in her heart as if her blood had drained away from the organ. She raised her hand to her chest in an automatic gesture.

A look of fear crossed Andy's face.

"Are you all right?"

Molly dropped her hand back down, not wanting to panic anyone.

"Yes, I'm fine. It was simply an impulse. It meant nothing." She assessed the almost exhilarating sensation of her heart skipping a beat. This feeling was different than the first time. It was less ripping and more like a tiny air bubble rising slowly in the center of her heart until it dissipated. Was it empathy for Andy? Was his heart breaking as he watched Becky disappear in the distance?

Molly studied Maria standing there in disarray. She smiled too fetchingly at Andy.

Maria ignored the fact that, whatever had happened in the barn, it had caused a rift between Andy and his girlfriend that would be tough to heal, if the pain ever went away. *Or was that what she wanted?*

Molly had to wonder, *is this girl evil? Will we regret the day we took her in? Surely, Andy must be judging that now, as well.*

Maria wobbled the empty bucket by its bail toward Andy. She smiled sweetly as she tossed her head to throw her long black hair back from her face. Andy reached out for the handle. Maria slid her hand up the wire, to touch Andy's fingers, as he took the pail from her.

Andy grasped the bail tighter, nearly jerking the bucket from Maria's hand, and stomped back to the barn. If there was to be any milk for the babies, tonight, he'd have to be the one to see to that. How he got himself out of this mess with Becky was beyond him.

Maria turned and rushed to follow him.

When she caught up, she yanked the pail back out of his hand.

"You go to the house. I'll milk the cow. It is my job. What do you think, I am stupid or something? I have been milking goats since I was five. How can a cow be any different?"

Andy looked at her with shock registering in his brain.

"Then why did you make me try to teach you?"

"You foolish *gringo*! You must learn when a girl wants attention from a man. Your friend that rode away so fast, she draws your eye, no? Then why do not I? Why must I pretend to be so helpless in order to get you to spend a few minutes with me?"

They reached the barn and Andy removed a lantern from its nail on the wall. Inside, the barn was darker than the twilight outside. He lit the wick and closed the globe over the flame.

He puzzled over Maria's words. *Did Becky realize how Maria felt? Had she come to the house because of jealousy and then found what she thought was proof of her distrust?*

"You can leave now," Maria told Andy curtly as she took the lantern from his hand. She made her way to the stanchion where Bossy still stood chewing her cud. The cow looked back at her as she approached with the bucket. Maria paused and hung the lantern nearby.

Andy turned without further comment. If she wanted to be left alone, he would comply.

Maria heard his footsteps diminish as the sound they made on the barn's wooden floor quieted when he stepped outside onto the ground. Andy made his way to the corral to close the horses in for the night.

Maria was alone.

She picked up the milking stool and set it beside the cow. Positioning herself comfortably alongside Bossy's rotund belly, she stripped the milk from the cow's udder until it sang into the bucket. The tone softened as the pail filled.

As Maria set up a rhythm, pulling milk with both hands, an uneasy feeling crept over her.

The hair on the back of her neck prickled. Bossy moved her hooves nervously about in the loose bedding hay. Her right rear foot kicked at the bucket with a loud clang and Maria grabbed the edge of the pail to keep the milk from dumping.

She rose and moved the bucket away from the cow while she checked the stanchion. She patted Bossy's neck and talked soothingly to her.

Did the cow hear something she didn't? What was out there?

Has Jesus come back to snatch me again? She looked over her shoulder, trying to make out any threat in the shadows.

In a dark corner of the barn, away from the lanterns

glow, Rosie crawled across the hay on all fours. She felt the urge to stalk Maria not as a kitten, this time, but as a full-grown cat. She was no longer Rosie. She was a mountain lion in search of prey. She lifted her palms feeling them now as the weight and size of a panther's enormous paws. Her fingers felt the sensation of fur tufts between them. She growled in a low, throaty, tone. It was only audible enough to prickle the hair on Maria's neck once more.

Rosie, pacing about on all fours, looked back over her shoulder seeing tawny fur instead of calico on her torso. She paced on hands and knees across the hay in the loft, then back again to sit on her buttocks and watch the girl below through the opening where the ladder reached from bottom to top floor.

Maria, fighting her apprehension, wanted to lurch from the barn. Instead, she denied the urge and talked to Bossy in soft, but shaky, tones.

"It is all right, Bossy. There's nothing here to hurt us." She spoke nervously to the cow as she tried also to convince herself.

Callie, Rosie's full-grown calico cat, slunk toward Maria. She purred loudly as she walked.

"See, Bossy, it is only *el gato*. Come, Callie," Maria snapped her fingers softly, calling the cat to her side.

Callie took up a position nearby, anticipating the taste of milk on her whiskers. When Andy milked the cow, he always made sure to squirt milk in Callie's face, aiming for her mouth and keeping the cat busy licking her paw and washing the fur on her muzzle to get the taste of the warm froth on her tongue.

On the floor was a chipped dish. Callie waited patiently for the milking to be finished and the warm white liquid to fill the dish from the bucket.

Maria relaxed feeling certain the noise she had heard was only Callie coming for her evening meal.

"Soon, Callie. I see your dish. I'll give you your dinner in a bit."

Rosie raised to a crouch and crept toward the loft opening watching Maria and Callie beneath her.

Suddenly, she dropped to the hay below near Maria. She hissed and flung her arm at Maria. She was a big cat swiping a paw at her prey.

Maria screamed, then recovered her composure.

"Rosie! You startled me! What are you doing?"

Rosie said nothing. She simply cowered and silently slunk away.

She stood upright at the barn door and walked slowly toward the house as Andy burst toward her with the rifle.

"What was that?"

"What?"

"We heard a scream. Was that you, Rosie?"

"No."

Rosie continued walking toward the house.

"Maria, are you all right?" Andy called out from the entrance to the barn.

"Yes," her voice quaked back. *What had Rosie been up to?* She had never seen someone act so strangely.

"I-I screamed because Rosie surprised me. I didn't know she had come out to the barn."

"I'll finish this up. You go on into the house." Andy set the rifle in the corner of the stall. He reached his hand over and rubbed the top of Callie's head. He felt the softness of her ear between his thumb and tip of his index finger.

Relief flushed over Maria. She handed Andy the nearly full pail. She would be glad to be back inside the warm kitchen with other people. If she milked again, she would be sure it was before nightfall. The expanse of the barn was far too ominous for her.

Seven

The roiling waters had separated Jesus and Maria and then deposited them each out at different ends of the dry creek beds, sparing both their lives. Maria had ended up at the end of the left bank of the creek fork, closer to the Westerman property. Jesus was washed down to the end of the right fork. The triangulation put more distance between him and Moriarty.

When Jesus finally picked himself up from a remote branch of the creek, where the flash flood had split him from his horse, he had searched for Maria.

He had risen slowly from the fan of gravel where the water splayed across the flat desert.

His horse, a slow, poor specimen of an animal, had quickly stopped fighting the foaming water and had slipped beneath the rushing current. Jesus, somewhat more determined to live, had managed to keep his head above water. The foaming brown liquid finally ran from the arroyo and flowed across the desert floor in a shallow temporary lake amidst the wide expanse of cactus and sagebrush before it soaked into the dry ground.

While he spent an hour, there, drying in the sun and

recovering from the shock and terror of near drowning, he had time to think about his actions. The wicked course of his life became evident to him. Not that he would change any of it but, he knew, he must never be caught and made to pay for his transgressions or, the next time, death would be certain—and quite possibly at the hands of Reyes.

When he felt he had regained enough of his strength, he had crept along the edge of the gully looking for any of his belongings. There was no sign of the horse, its tack, or any of his supplies. There was no sign of Maria.

He called out, weakly, a few times.

"Maria! Maria! Maria!"

No answer came back.

He then set off on foot, hoping to come across a means to find her and to put more miles between him and Reyes. He knew Reyes would come after them. He would not stop until he reclaimed his little sister—dead or alive. And, if she was dead, Jesus would soon be, too.

The thought made him move faster and he felt a twist in his gut that sent him heading to the nearby brush with diarrhea.

Holy Mother of Jesus! How do I get myself into such trouble? Not being a man of God, he wondered at his own words. Atheist or not, he would have to call upon all the saints and all that was Holy, if Reyes caught up to him.

To his amazement at his own luck, he found the flash flood had dumped him out a few yards from a lonely cabin. As he scanned the horizon, he could see three horses grazing not far from the rough shack. If he were very cautious, perhaps he could sneak up close enough to walk one of the animals away. If he could, he might also be able to steal some food to satisfy his growling stomach.

Jesus sidled up close to the horses. They paid him no attention as they continued to snip at the low-cropped, sparse clumps of prairie grass.

He moved past them and edged to a hole, cut in the side of the tiny cabin, which served as a window. He could smell the odor of rancid bacon grease hanging heavy in the air as he looked inside through the window. When he peered further, he heard snoring. He saw the remains of fried potatoes spread in small crumbles across a dirty tin plate on a makeshift table. A man slept on the floor on top of his bedroll next to the rough-hewn legs of the lopsided table.

Jesus thought carefully. He could go into the cabin and try to find something to eat. If he did, and the man woke up, he would have no weapon to defend himself. The man gripped his six-shooter tightly in his right fist where it lay across his chest.

Jesus slumped against the outside wall and slowly slid down the wood until he sat on his heels contemplating his dilemma.

He crawled on his hands and knees around the back of the building. There he found a small pile of garbage containing wrinkled potato peelings and onion skins amidst discarded coffee grounds. He dug his fingers into the trash, pulling the scraps to his mouth and chewing rapidly at the dried peelings. Why the man hadn't cooked his potatoes, skins and all, was a wonder to Jesus but he was thankful for the small bits of nourishment. He found a moldy piece of onion and scraped away the gray dust, as best he could, before cramming it into his mouth.

The morsels were not enough to completely satisfy his hunger, but they would be sufficient to keep him alive a bit longer. He slipped back away from the cabin toward the grazing horses.

He chose the best horse and raised his hand to rub its nose. The odor of onions on his fingers concealed the scent of a stranger and the horse bobbed its head slightly. Jesus twined his fingers into the horse's dark mane and swung himself onto its tan-colored back.

Slowly, he edged it away from the pasture and its companions.

Alert, now, the other two horses nickered curiously at the third.

Jesus' stolen mount answered back.

He urged it on more quickly.

The other horses set up a whinnying chorus.

Suddenly, the man appeared at the cabin door, dazed and half asleep. Groggy, he slowly raised his arm and aimed the pistol in Jesus' direction.

Jesus kicked the horse in its ribs, spurring it away from the cabin, back toward the arroyo where he hoped the lower land would seclude him.

He heard the pop of the gun and a bullet zinged past his head. He dropped low on the horse and kicked its sides harder.

Night was falling and he hoped, if the man rode after him, it would soon be too dark for him to follow his trail.

Jesus rode on into the night, not stopping until he reached the spot he judged to be the area where the flashflood had swept Maria from her horse and him downstream.

He stopped and listened intently for his pursuer.

When he heard nothing, he dismounted and settled in to sleep. Tomorrow, he would look for Maria again—thinking, by now, all he would find was her corpse.

~ * ~

The next morning, Jesus led the horse by its mane while he walked the banks of the creek where he had last seen Maria. He looked for any sign of the girl.

He kicked a metal pot with his toe and recognized it as one of the utensils he had carried in his pack.

Encouraged by that, he moved on, touching the ground and reading what information he found there in animal prints and scraps of debris. He came upon an area where the bank sloped upward. Something appeared to have pulled itself across the mud and up the bank from the water.

There was a small circle where talons had gripped the soft dirt and buzzard feathers lay stuck in the mud.

He felt the earth, looking for bones or a skull. He found nothing.

Did Maria die here? Did the buzzards pick her bones clean and the coyotes drag them away?

He felt a gnawing in the pit of his stomach that far exceeded the sensation of hunger.

He fell to his knees and patted the now dried mud, searching for anything that would confirm or deny his suspicions.

As he studied the fine sandy earth he saw where someone, or something, had either been dragged, or dragged itself, away from the buzzards' feeding circle. He followed the trail until he lost it in the low prairie grass.

He stood staring off into the distance, looking in all directions, to determine where Maria's body, or what was left of it, might be.

His eyes honed in on the distant farmhouse.

He was near Moriarty. He recognized the farm as one where he had stolen a beautiful black horse for Maria. He had set fire to the *gringo's* barn, to slow him down, a couple years back. Apparently, the *gringo,* and his family, had managed to save the building, or rebuild it, and cling to their hold on the land. He could see a small herd of cattle in the pasture. Everything seemed peaceful.

He made his way toward the farm and rode the fence line slowly and cautiously. It was evening and the day was dimming. He saw figures in the distance moving from the barn to the house.

Maria! He would know her form anywhere. *It was Maria.* She approached the *niño*. Then a second person mounted a horse and rode out in haste. *Perhaps all is not so calm after all.*

Undetected, he dismounted and watched the small scene play out before him. He studied the lay of the land, the setting of the buildings. He searched his mind trying to figure how he could snatch Maria again.

When darkness fell, and the glow from the kerosene lights inside the house went out, Jesus, having his bearings once more, rode toward Moriarty.

A short distance outside of town, he wove grass blades into a flimsy thong to hobble the horse. It wouldn't be good to get caught in town with a horse lacking any form of tack and someone else's brand on its rump. Someone might question if it were stolen. The sheriff didn't take kindly to horse thieves here, he knew from his past experience. The posse would hunt him down and hang him, if he were caught, he was sure. The horse he had taken for Maria had almost cost him his life. He had been lucky to make it back to Mexico before the *gringos* caught him, no thanks to her brother Reyes.

With the horse secure in the dark, he went into town and paced the wooden sidewalk slowly. His stomach growled. He hadn't eaten since the potato peelings and onion skins a full day before.

He walked behind a boarding house looking for kitchen scraps. There in a bucket were meat bones and eggshells amidst a pile of coffee grounds. A vicious dog had already beaten him to the container and was laying claim to its contents.

"Grrrrrr!" The dog bared its teeth and threatened Jesus.

Jesus backed away and tripped over the edge of the sidewalk. He sprawled across the boards and fell flat on his face, knocking the wind from his lungs. He lay there, stunned, for a moment.

As his breathing became normal, again, he saw a coin exposed in the dim light coming from the open door of a boarding house that served food to its clientele. He could not believe his good fortune!

He picked the money up and studied the denomination, considering whether to go inside and order something to eat or move on down the street to the nearest saloon and buy a drink.

His desire for a strong shot of *tequila* overpowered his need for food and he rose to his feet and crossed the street to the saloon.

Jesus purchased a half-empty bottle of the liquor and situated himself in a dark corner of the room. He sipped the drink slowly from the bottle's neck instead of using a glass. He relished the burning sensation that ran down his throat and into his empty stomach.

He was a happy man. He was glad to be alive. He was glad that he would have another chance to try, once more, to claim Maria for his own. Thoughts of Reyes, and what he might do to him, were totally out of his mind.

He dozed in the warmth of the alcohol, tilting back in his chair and feeling all the sensations of being alive while the slats of the chair back cradled his body like a baby's bed.

Then, suddenly, the cold steel of a pistol jabbed the soft flesh beneath his chin bringing him to attention.

The click of a gun cocking echoed through the hushed room.

"Where's Maria?" Reyes growled.

"Reyes. Heh, heh, heh. Careful, *mi amigo*. You don't want to kill Jesus."

"Talk fast you lousy son of a coyote. Where is my little sister?"

"I have nothing to do with whatever is happening to Maria."

"You lie, you coyote."

"Take down your *pistola* and I will tell you what I know."

Reyes thought for a moment, then relaxed the hammer letting the barrel hit against Jesus' jawbone roughly as he removed it.

"It is that *gringo* homesteader and his family. They

have Maria. They have made a slave of her. I found her on their farm but there was no time to get her and there were too many of them. I could do nothing but wait for you to come and help me save her."

"If what you tell me is true, the *gringos* will die."

"Have I not always been truthful with you, Reyes?"

Reyes cocked his left eyebrow.

Eight

Andy had been in the barn for only a few minutes, stripping the milk from the cow's teats to finish the milking Maria had started, when he sensed someone behind him.

Perhaps Becky has returned? Well, if she had, he wasn't about to turn around and rush toward her and encircle her in his arms in an instant. For all he cared, she could stand there and consider her lack of trust in him. Maybe it was time she learned a lesson.

He compressed the flesh of the cow's teat between his thumb and forefinger, again, and watched the stream of milk hit the white pool in the bucket. The milk sang against the inside of the metal pail like a melody as he pulled and released, pulled and released.

What is up with Becky? Is she trying to outwait me? Is she trying to make me be the one to apologize when she was the one to jump to conclusions?

"Meow." Callie pleaded for another squirt of milk in the face.

Andy aimed the stream in her direction.

The cow's udder was nearly empty, now, and he had plenty of milk in the bucket to feed the babies and to leave the cat a generous portion.

He concentrated on hitting Callie square on the lips with the milk.

"Ah, *niño*, I told you we would meet again. You have grown. You have nearly become a man."

The words sent a chill down Andy's spine. It had been a long time since he had heard the voice—since he had been called a "*niño*."

There was only one person in the world that called him that. And, the word bespoke a threat. He shuddered. Releasing the cow's teats, he rose slowly and turned, reaching for the rifle.

"No, *niño*." Reyes kicked the rifle butt away with his boot.

"What are you doing here?"

"Ah, *niño*, you are not happy to see me? I wonder why. Could it be that you have been doing something you shouldn't? Could it be that you have my little sister?"

Reyes studied the young man before him. He had gotten taller. He was much better looking than he had been the last time they met. *He might be someone who could take advantage of my little sister, if I was not around to protect her.*

"No. Maria was injured. She came to us for help. I have done nothing to harm her."

"Then why did you not send word to my family that she was safe?"

"We didn't know she was your sister. Trace and I

94

found her all beat up and nearly dead. We brought her home and Molly and Rosie nursed her back to health. Doc Landry told them what to do to help her and gave her medicine."

"Set the bucket down, *niño*. We are going to the house and get my sister. If you have harmed her, I will tear you apart piece by piece. If you have fooled around with my little sister, I will cut your heart out and give it to her. Now, walk slowly and quietly toward the house."

Andy did as he was told, all the while trying to figure a way to warn Trace and the rest of the family of the danger coming in.

Reyes sensed that Andy was hesitating.

"Don't even think to run. I will shoot you where you stand."

Andy shrugged. "I hadn't planned to."

The front door of the house opened. Trace stood looking out into the night, silhouetted by the light of the flickering kerosene lamp. His rifle in his hand, he searched the darkness for Andy.

"Andy, are you about through with the milking?" Trace called out toward the barn.

Reyes slipped into the shadows.

"Answer calmly. I am right here and my gun is aimed at your back."

"Yes, Pa. I'm through."

"Then, what's keeping you? The babies are waiting for their milk."

"I left the bucket in the barn. I have to go back and get it. I'll be right there."

Trace turned and shut the door.

What is wrong with that boy? He isn't normally so forgetful. Is he sidetracked by these two girls?

If Reyes were to get Maria without harming her in the process, he'd need the element of surprise. He didn't want to have a shootout with Trace Westerman. *The gringo is too good.* He had seen his work. He was smart and accurate with his guns. Reyes wasn't about to fire into the house and perhaps hit Maria in the exchange of gunfire.

Reyes knew if he were to get close to the house, Andy would need the milk pail.

"Be quick about it. Get the pail and return. Remember, I am right behind you."

When they reached the house, again, Reyes instructed Andy further.

"Stop where you are. Call Maria out to the barn and go back there. If you don't want your *madre* or one of the *niños* hurt, do as I say."

"Here's the milk," Andy shouted toward the door. "I forgot something. I'll be right back."

Trace came through the door, picked up the bucket and returned inside the house, shutting the door behind him.

"I told you to call Maria out," Reyes said with anger deepening his voice when Andy turned.

"And how would that look? Don't you think my Pa and Ma would wonder what I was up to?"

Reyes thought for a moment.

"So, you will come with me until I can figure out a way to get Maria safely away from the house."

The sound of a group of riders, their horses' hooves

pounding the earth rapidly, reached Andy and Reyes.

The striking of horse shoes on dry hard-packed earth became louder and louder as the riders entered the lane to the house.

Reyes swiped at Andy to grab his arm, but Andy was too quick and spun away. He raced toward the noise the horses made, thinking Reyes surely wouldn't shoot him where he might get chased down himself by the riders.

"I'll be back, *niño!*" Reyes' voice was a loud whisper as he ran toward the barn.

Trace, with Molly and the children following closely behind, rushed to the front porch.

Reyes slunk into the barn and made his way out the back door. He hesitated at the opening to listen for an explanation to the commotion.

"Whoa!" The voices called to their steeds to stop as they reined up in front of Trace and the family. Andy moved quickly to their side, bounding the steps of the porch in one fast lunge.

"What's going on, Sheriff?" Trace asked lowering the barrel of his rifle toward the ground when he recognized the lead man.

"We're searching for a horse thief. You seen anyone riding a horse without any tack and I mean not even a bridle? He's some Mexican that looks like he's been drug behind a horse for a ways."

"No." Trace answered back.

A shiver went down Maria's arms to her fingertips. She rubbed her hands along her arms to warm the chill.

"Excuse me, Miss. Didn't mean no disrespect," the

sheriff said mistaking Maria's shiver of anxiety for one of taking offense at what might be prejudice.

Maria studied the boards on the porch.

The posse's horses fidgeted as they waited to be let loose into a full run again.

Rosie headed the younger children back into the house. Maria followed.

Could it be Jesus? Maria glanced from the kitchen window and saw a shadow move across the side of the barn. Was that why she had been so jumpy when she was milking? Had Jesus been stalking her all this time? Was it only a coincidence that Callie and Rosie showed up?

Maria reached down and picked Emmy up from the floor.

"Let's see if we can get one of those dollies made before you have to go to bed, little *señorita*."

She carried the little girl to the rug in front of the fireplace and sat her amidst wooden clothes pins, fabric scraps and buttons.

Outside, the riders turned their mounts and moved away from the porch before releasing the horses into a full-speed run.

Trace, Andy and Molly returned inside.

"Seth, did you shut the chickens up?" Molly asked when she saw him standing against the fireplace watching the girls with curiosity. Crazy Leg sat next to his feet, tilting his head as if he, too, was trying to figure out what they were doing.

"Yes, Ma."

"You're sure? You forgot last night. Maybe you better

go check."

"No!" Andy said too abruptly, causing Trace to look at him sharply.

"I'll take care of it tonight," Andy added more calmly.

Molly took Jacob from Rosie so the girl could start washing the dishes from dinner. Callie twined herself between Rosie's legs, dragging her tail leisurely along her bare calves. She purred loudly. Baby Jacob strained away from Molly and stretched his arm down, trying to reach the tip of Callie's tail.

"Save a plate of food for Andy. His chores took so long he's probably near starving. Sorry, Andy, we would have waited for you but the food was getting cold and I didn't think you'd get here in time before the babies got sleepy."

"I told Molly you wouldn't mind eating a warmed over supper," Trace added. "Sometimes that happens when a man has work to do."

Crazy Leg left Seth's side abruptly. He moved through the kitchen and whined at the door, then scratched the edge to get back out.

Seth hurried to oblige.

"Stop that, Crazy Leg. Ma doesn't want the door frame clawed up. You'll get us both in trouble."

"Didn't you feed that dog either, Seth?" Molly's voice reminded him he had neglected some of his duties lately.

"I was just going to." Seth turned from the door and hurried to the get Crazy Leg's bowl and scoop leftovers into it.

The food being put into his dish distracted the dog from what he sensed was going on outside. He whined and looked at the door, then back at Seth and the food. When Seth set the bowl on the floor, Crazy Leg dropped a small piece of metal, he had found earlier in the yard, from his mouth. It clinked softly on the rag rug Molly kept on the floor beneath the table that served as a counter for washing dishes and preparing food, then, catching the edge, it rolled off the rug and under the still-hot cook stove.

Seth got down on his hands and knees, using care not to get too close to the hot metal, to retrieve the object.

"What cha got there, Crazy Leg?" Seth whispered, rubbing the dog's scruff.

He picked the object up and wove it between his fingers. The dog's slobbers were still on it and he wiped the metal across his pants leg before he inspected it. It was a smooth, round piece of silver that was fluted on its edges. The *concho* had two holes in the center where a leather thong could be threaded through it to attach it to another object. It appeared to be something that might have been on chaps or a vest at one time.

Seth fingered it some more, then slipped it into his pants pocket. He tilted his head down on top of Crazy Leg's skull and rubbed his silky ear fur with the other hand.

Molly and Trace were busy playing with Jacob. Trace, holding Callie, now, was using the tip of the cat's tail to tickle Jacob's nose.

Jacob giggled. He squeezed his eyes shut and tossed his head back as he sputtered bubbles from his pursed lips.

Andy stood near the door waiting for Trace to stop the

play so he could signal him to come outside.

"Well, I guess I better go help Andy make certain everything is closed up outside," he told Molly seeing Andy fidgeting near the door. He reached for his rifle and six-shooter. Andy was far too nervous for his taste. *Something must be making him edgy. Something Andy doesn't want the women and children to know about.*

Andy stuck close to Trace as they went onto the porch.

When they were far enough away from the house he spoke in a low voice, "Reyes was here. He says Maria's his sister. He thinks we're holding her against her will."

"What? Why would he think that?"

"I don't know, but he sure was mad and he accused me of all sorts of things."

Trace moved the lever of the rifle, feeding a bullet into the chamber. He cradled it between his side and his elbow while he pulled his pistol from where he had stuck it in the waistband of his pants. He popped the cylinder aside to make sure the bullets were loaded in all the chambers. He snapped the gun back together, spun the cylinder and kept it in his hand.

He glanced anxiously back toward the house.

"Reyes approached me in the barn. Then he was going to make me get Maria out there, but the posse scared him off, I think."

"We don't need any more trouble from that man. If Maria's his sister, we'll have to see that she is returned to him."

They stopped at the small chicken coop and Trace stood guard while Andy checked the latch. Seth had spoken the truth. The chickens were snug on their roost and Andy could hear their light rustlings as they settled into sleep.

They went on into the barn and Trace took the still lit lantern down from its nail while Andy released Bossy from the stanchion. There hadn't been a chance to turn the cow loose earlier and she looked at him as if he had been remiss in his duties. Andy opened another stall away from the milking area to keep the cow inside for the night. He made sure there was plenty of hay in the feed box and added a bit more grain.

Trace latched the back barn door and then the two of them made their way back out into the yard in front of the barn.

"Better not say anything to Molly, or anyone else, until we figure out just what is going on."

Andy agreed.

"I can't believe that the horse thief was Reyes. But, who knows. Apparently, he didn't stick around when the posse rode in," Trace said.

"He'll be back. He said he would."

"And, I believe he will. Once we get to the bottom of this, we'll have to tell Maria. She needs to return to her home."

She's sure starting to cause a lot of trouble around here! Trace thought, mulling over the events of the evening. Of course, he understood her brother's desire to retrieve his sister. With the past history between Reyes and himself, he could understand that he wouldn't walk up to the door and knock. But, there surely was some other way to handle things than to come prowling around a fella's home, like a thief in the night, and toss threats around.

He had still been upset when he found out the trouble Maria had caused between Becky and Andy. He was trying to be the polite host and not let Maria know how much her actions bothered him. Trace had enough to worry about with his own family. *If Maria does have a home to go to, that's where she* belongs. *It was important that she go there as soon as possible.*

Nine

"Trace," Molly called from the house.

"We'll be right there, Molly."

"Will you help me for a moment?"

"Sure. Andy has to finish taking care of Comet. Then we'll both be there."

"You go ahead," Andy said. "The lantern is still lit. I'll put it out before I come."

Trace gave him a questioning look in the dim light.

"I'm sure it's all right. The animals are settled down. That's a good sign nobody's around, right?"

"Usually," Trace agreed.

"We haven't seen anything to indicate Reyes is here, now," Andy added.

The kid is making more sense than I am, Trace thought.

"The posse probably did scare him off," Trace agreed. "And, I'm sure he'll come back—as long as Maria is here. We have to figure some way to get her to him."

"Trace—," Molly called again.

"I won't be far behind," Andy assured him.

"See that you're not. I don't like what's been going on here tonight."

~ * ~

Trace became uneasy once he was inside the house. He tried to hide his concern from Molly while he helped her ready the younger children for bed. Fifteen minutes passed and no Andy. He looked out the bedroom window and saw the glow the lantern emitted across the barnyard from the open door. Surely, he would be here soon.

When an hour had passed and Andy didn't come back from the barn, Trace went looking for him.

"Andy," he called out. His name echoed back in a dull tone to him.

He searched the barn, checking each stall and climbing to the hayloft when he didn't find him on the main floor. He called out his name, once more. When there was no response, he went back down the ladder to the main section of the barn. Andy had gone to bring Comet in when he left him. Now, he realized when he had checked the stalls, the horse was not there. He couldn't tell if Andy had ever put him in the stall. The bedding hay appeared undisturbed. There was no way to track him on the wooden floor.

The lantern, still lit, hung on a nail in a timber above the gate to Comet's stall. Trace removed it and carried it to the back door. He raised it high to look out, as far as possible into the darkness, then lowered it as he stooped to search for hoof prints.

There, where the dirt met the barn door sill, he saw Comet's prints and followed them a short distance. Soon the prints of a second horse joined those of the first and led off through the back corral and out the gate. Again, he raised his arm high overhead and searched as far as the lamplight would allow. There was no sign of Comet or Andy. *Who was riding the second horse?* He suspected it was Reyes.

Trace returned to the house with the bad news for Molly.

"I can't track them at night. There's no point in even trying. Whoever Andy rode off with, finding them will have to wait until morning." He didn't want to mention the possibility it was Reyes and worry Molly worse than the concern that already showed on her face.

Molly's fear for Andy became frantic. She paced the floor.

"Molly, stay calm. We'll get him home. Andy's a smart boy. He can take care of himself," Trace tried to reassure her.

"I'm not so sure about that. Maybe, if he rode out alone, but, with someone else? Why, it could be that horse thief the sheriff was looking for."

"I'm sure neither of us will get much sleep tonight. I'll ride out at daybreak." Trace put his arm around Molly and whispered in her ear.

"We're frightening Rosie."

Molly looked at the girl. She tried to calm her own agitation and moved to sit in the rocking chair alongside the fireplace.

When Trace followed Molly from the kitchen, Rosie shrank within herself. She crawled behind the cook stove. There, she disturbed Callie where she was already curled into a cozy ball. The cat stretched and moved onto her back kneading her paws in the air and purring. Rosie pulled her knees up beneath her nightgown and rolled herself into a semi-circle around the cat.

The heat from cooking the evening meal was fast diminishing from the stove, but Rosie found comfort there. She didn't know what she would do when she grew too big to safely nestle there in her times of trouble as she had been doing lately.

Crazy Leg went to the front door and whined.

Trace moved to let the dog out.

Maria lay on the pillows in the living room.

"We better get some rest, too. I'll have a hard ride in the morning trying to catch up to Andy." Trace reached out and hugged Molly.

"Come on. I know you probably won't sleep, but you need to go to bed instead of sitting here worrying."

Crazy Leg was back to scratch at the door before they left the kitchen.

Molly sighed and opened the door to let the dog in.

He moved up the stairs in search of Seth.

~ * ~

Reyes reined his horse toward the mountain.

"*Niño*, keep up with me."

"If Maria's your sister, all you have to do is ride up and tell Pa and Ma and take her home with you," Andy suggested. He didn't see the need for dragging him off and making him follow all the way to the mountain.

Reyes had been waiting for him when he went to the corral to lead Comet inside the barn. They hadn't gotten across the threshold before Reyes had reached out of the darkness and clutched the horse's mane.

"Do you think your *gringo padre* would even let me get close to that house? If he knew I was anywhere around, he'd be strapping his guns on."

"He knows. I told him before we returned to the barn. Let me go back and arrange something with him to let Maria meet you somewhere. He'll really come after you, once he finds me missing again."

"That is a chance I have to take. Maybe I can trade you for Maria and there might not be a killing. I have to think. What is best to do?"

In the distance, Andy heard a cougar scream. They couldn't be far from the mountain now. The big cats didn't like to come down into the valley unless food was scarce. It had been bountiful and there was no reason for them to poach the homesteaders' livestock. Andy got a sick feeling in his stomach. At least Reyes was thinking about exchanging him for Maria. That was a ray of hope. In the meantime, he'd have to try to think of a way to escape, in case Reyes changed his mind. He didn't trust this man. His past experiences with him had not been the best.

Andy picked up another sound, now. It was a distant, steady beat of the hooves of a single horse. Was his Pa already coming after him? He began to jabber at Reyes, hoping he had not heard the horse. He hoped he would not hear it, if he continued to talk.

"Hush, *niño*," Reyes ordered. He stopped his horse and listened, then reached back and pulled Comet's reins from Andy's hands.

"We must race away." He spurred his horse ahead, nearly jerking Andy off Comet as the horse jumped to follow.

~ * ~

In the dark, with only the pale light of the moon to guide him, a lone rider kept his horse at a steady pace down the center of the wagon road leading across the Estancia Valley. He was careful not to let the animal gain too much speed, trying to avoid the possibility of a misstep that would land the animal's hoof in a hole and cause him to have to shoot him and go on afoot.

He cared about his horse and having to kill it would be worse than having to walk, so he began to slow his pace and use more caution.

It had been a long ride from Waco, Texas and he was tired and wanted to get on into Moriarty and rest before meeting with the town's sheriff.

From habit, he felt the metal badge on his left vest pocket with his right fingertips. He brushed his left hand across the mother-of-pearl handle of his six-shooter at his left hip to assure himself it was still there. Perhaps it was a bit of vanity that made him carry a gun with a pearl face on the butt but he liked the way the colors showed, like a summer rainbow, when he polished it with a soft cloth. There was little in this life to bring joy. He couldn't keep much in the way of possessions in the job he had. His gun and a change of clothes, maybe a new hat now and then, were about it. *Texas Rangers don't need much, not when they're on the trail most of the time.*

He remembered this part of New Mexico from the last time he had been assigned to infiltrate a gang of outlaws here and bring them to justice. He remembered, not far ahead, on the right, was the Kling farm. It was owned by a woman homesteader with three kids, the last he knew. Trace Westerman had been helping them get a grip on the land and rode with him to Texas in search of the oldest kid's black horse when it was stolen by one of Reyes Espiañata's *vaqueros*. But that had been a while back, he calculated, and he didn't know what had happened to Westerman after they parted company in Texas. Maybe he stayed there, for all he knew. He doubted it though. He knew Trace would have seen to it the kid got his horse back.

Tom Jennings looked off into the dark landscape, his eyes searching in the direction of the Kling property to see if there were lights lit in a house now. He saw a slight glimmer. Then the light went out. If a house sat there, the family must have turned in for the night. *No point in disturbing them.* He turned his horse to the left and aimed for another three-mile ride on into Moriarty.

~ * ~

The Westerman's house quieted as each found their place of rest for the night. Rosie clutched Callie in her arms and crawled out from behind the stove and climbed the stairs to her bed. She had seen Seth pick something up off the floor beneath the stove. She thought it must have been a button Maria dropped when she was making doll clothes for Emmy. She paid him no never mind as she had been getting sleepy and wanted nothing more than to curl up like Callie and call it a day. She worried about Andy, but there was nothing she could do but wait and pray. Trace would have to be the one to do anything beyond that.

Maria, appearing to be asleep to the others, lay running the events of the day through her mind. *Who had taken Andy? Had Jesus returned? Was it Reyes? Why hadn't he just come for me if he was the one that spirited Andy away?*

She heard the small rustlings of Trace, Molly and the younger children settling in for the night in the rooms upstairs as she courted sleep where she had decided to stay on the living room pillows. She was in that hazy moment, right before dropping off, when she felt a hand slip across her mouth.

"Don't scream!" A voice whispered.

She struggled, but strong arms held her tight.

The man lifted her up from the floor and dragged her, quietly, across the darkened room.

She tried to grip his hand with her teeth but he managed to avoid the pinch.

"Be still." The voice whispered as the man used his other hand to open the front door and edge her outside. "Do you want to get the others killed?"

Who would have the nerve to come inside the house with everyone asleep upstairs? Jesus? He is a coward. Where is that crazy dog? Maria wondered. *Why hasn't he woke up the entire family? Why wasn't he attacking the intruder?*

Now she was out in the yard and still no Crazy Leg. *What has the man done with him?*

"You yell and I'll knock you out with my pistol to your head," Jesus threatened as he shoved her onto the horse where she would sit in front of him. "Don't expect the dog to help you, either. I saw him go back into the house. He's probably sound asleep with the kid."

It is Jesus!

She tried to spur her bare heels into the horse's sides

and leave Jesus behind but he was too quick and was astride the horse behind her before it lurched away.

"What are you doing with me? Reyes will kill you, yet."

"Reyes is no where to be found. I saw him ride off with the *niño*. He will be surprised when he comes back and you are no longer here."

"You will be surprised when he catches up with you!"

Jesus laughed in her ear.

"Reyes will never find us. There is a job waiting for us somewhere where no one knows us. You and me, we will be in charge of the rancher's cookhouse. Reyes will never think to look there. By then, you will be my wife. Reyes would surely never kill his brother-in-law."

Ten

Tom Jennings reached Moriarty late in the night and, having missed dinner, let his growling stomach lead him to one of the saloons. With luck, there'd be a piece of meat and some bread there if the bartender hadn't already sold out.

He flipped his badge inside his vest pocket beneath the outer flap of the smooth brown-stained cowhide before he entered the swinging doors.

Always vigilant, Tom's eyes scanned the dim room. He saw no one he recognized, good or bad, and moved to the bar.

"Got anything left to eat?"

"There's some beans and bread, if you're interested in that."

"I'm hungry enough, it don't much matter what it is. That'll be fine."

The bartender dished the food up and handed a plate, with boiled pinto beans and a chunk of stale bread on top, to Tom.

"Want anything to drink?"

"No. This'll do."

Tom moved to a nearby table and lifted a tipped-over chair back on its legs to sit down.

"Want some company, cowboy?" A woman that had moved close to his right elbow asked.

Tom looked up from his meal and studied her features. She was pretty, with a slightly plain look to her face, and long blond hair pulled back at the temples and caught somehow to fall with the rest of her long tresses onto her shoulders.

"No. I don't believe so. I just want to eat my food while it's hot and get a room to stay in for the night."

"I have a place."

He studied his beans, knowing they were cooling even while the woman drew his attention, and thought about her offer. He could be mean and tell her to leave him alone, but he carried a kinder heart than that and searched for a way to decline her nicely.

"No, I've got business to tend to. Maybe some other time." He scooped a mouthful of beans and chewed his food while he hoped she'd go away.

She lingered.

"Can I sit here for a while? That guy over there is giving me a bad time. I'm afraid to go back."

Tom nodded.

"Sure. I suppose some company might be nice, if you don't mind if I eat while you sit." Tom pulled one of the chairs up from another table. "Guess your sitting here won't do any harm." He glanced over his shoulder toward the man the girl had indicated.

She sat down and watched him eat his food.

He was famished and wanted to wolf the beans and bread down in a rush. But, to be polite, he paced himself and tried to pay attention to what the woman said.

When his appetite was sated enough, he asked between bites, "What keeps you working here? If you have a problem with the guy, why don't you leave?"

She let her eyelids shade her pupils as she studied her hands in her lap.

"It's all I know. Where else could I find a job?"

"Anything ought to beat takin' up with strangers. Like me. You don't know anything about me, yet, you came to me to protect you."

"You had a kind look. That guy over there—he's just plain mean."

"Who is he?" Tom wiped the bottom of his plate with the last bite of the bread and put it in his mouth.

"He rides with the Bennington gang. You've heard of them haven't you?"

"I'm not from around here." Tom wasn't about to provide any information he had if he could gain some from someone else. His words were not a lie, but an avoidance. He did know who the leader of the Bennington gang was. He thought about the paper in his vest pocket.

It contained orders from Ranger Headquarters. He had a specific job to do. The mission he was on was not to be interfered with.

Tom knew he had no official jurisdiction in New Mexico. Short of checking in with the sheriff, there was not a lot he could do about the woman's problem—unless the man made it personal. His own mission was to transport a prisoner from Albuquerque. One that was so mean and vicious that a jail wagon would be hauling him. Guarding the wagon, alone, Tom was to be the driver's escort back to Waco to make sure none of the outlaw's cronies broke him out. He was due in Albuquerque tomorrow and he didn't have time to get involved with this young woman or her problems.

If he had been in a location where he could, he would have taken his orders out of his pocket and read the prisoner's name, again, to make sure they were both talking about the same outlaw. If Rigor Bennington was the leader of the same gang, he needed to know if the man across the room was one of his men.

The man that had been tormenting the woman looked back. He studied Tom and the woman sitting next to him.

Tom heard a coarse whisper, "What cha goin' ta do, Smitty?"

"Ah, hell, nothin' I guess. Rigor said not to get into any trouble. I got one job to do and that's get him out before they can send him to Texas. He'd kill me if I messed up and ended up in jail over a woman. Now, money—that's a different story," he laughed coarsely and glared at Tom for interfering with his fun.

So, the man is one of Rigor's henchmen. Tom thanked his good fortune for being tipped off that trouble might lie ahead. He had known the job wouldn't be easy. The way things were turning out, he, at least, knew where trouble might come from now.

"Well, I have to be finding somewhere to sleep for the night. Can I walk you someplace?"

The woman considered her options. If she stayed at the saloon, the night could turn ugly.

"Yes, thank you. You can walk me to the boarding house where I live, if you don't mind. I don't want to take a chance on having to deal with that guy anymore tonight. Maybe he'll be gone tomorrow."

Tom wondered at her living in a boarding house instead of upstairs above the saloon. Perhaps he had misjudged her and she wasn't like most of the women he had seen in saloons. *She is a puzzle*, but he kept his curiosity to himself. He stood and took her hand to assist her to her feet. He moved his hand to her elbow and directed her through the bar's clientele. She stopped at the coat rack nailed to the wall beside the swinging doors and retrieved a long burgundy colored cape.

Tom took it from her hands and wrapped it around her shoulders. Its length fell to her ankles and, with the wrap covering the provocative dress she wore no one would have known where she had spent her evening. Tom held one of the doors open for her and they moved outside onto the boardwalk.

They strolled along the boardwalk beneath the overhanging store porch roofs where lanterns lit their way.

"It's up the street, a few more buildings, to where I

live. Maybe you could get a room for the night there, too."

"Maybe I could," Tom answered but, his thoughts were distracted by the man they had left behind in the saloon. He etched his face in his mind so he would know him, should he run into him again.

A few doors down, they came to the boarding house. The woman removed a skeleton key to unlock the door and reached to turn the doorknob.

"Here, let me," Tom offered.

They entered the parlor.

"I'll find Mrs. Swartz and send her out to discuss a room with you. Thank you, again, sir. Good night." The woman moved down a hall and disappeared.

Mrs. Swartz soon appeared, wearing a heavy robe and carrying a kerosene lamp to lead Tom to his room. She waited for him to light another lamp sitting on a bureau beside the bed before leaving him.

Tom thanked the woman and closed the door behind her. When he was alone, he sat down on the bed and removed his orders from his vest pocket. He unfolded the wrinkled paper and smoothed it out on the bureau top alongside the light.

> *Escort prisoner James (Rigor) Bennington from Albuquerque to Waco to stand trial on July 16.*

It was written in a heavy print on the paper.

It confirmed that he did have business with the man in the saloon, if the woman was right and he was one of

Bennington's men. He'd have to be cautious. Maybe the man was having what he thought was a good time. *And, maybe he has other plans,* Tom thought. *It certainly sounded that way.*

He cupped his palm above the lamp globe and blew out the flame. Tom unbuckled the belt to his holster and re-buckled it to hang it from the metal post of the headboard. He removed his vest and pulled off his boots. He lay down on his back, otherwise fully dressed, on top of the cover of the bed and crossed his arms and ankles. He would be prepared for whatever might come.

There was no telling what tomorrow would bring.

Eleven

When Reyes and Andy had made the trip safely up the mountainside and over the crest, Reyes tied Comet's reins to a tree limb and ordered Andy to dismount.

He tied his own horse alongside Comet and left the two horses to graze on what grass they could reach from under the tree while he searched for a good location to put a campfire.

"*Niño*, if you don't want to get cold tonight, gather some dry limbs and we will make a fire."

"Aren't you afraid someone will see us?"

"No, *niño*. That horse you heard back there has gone on up the valley. We are on the backside of the mountain. Anyone coming from the direction of your home will not see us. From this side? Well, we are two hunters out looking for *el gato*, no?"

Andy remembered the loud cry of the cat earlier in the evening and it made him nervous. He didn't expect it would attack them as there were two of them and, with a fire burning, it would surely stay away. That was enough incentive for him to begin gathering wood—lots of wood—to keep the fire burning all night.

The horses twitched their legs and rolled their eyes. Although they had probably heard the cat, as well, the smell of it frightened them.

Reyes was placing sections of stone in a circle. Andy could hear the distinct clinking of the shale.

"*Niño*, I am watching you. Do not go too far. Besides, *el gato* might get you," Reyes laughed ghoulishly.

Andy had seen a horse that had been attacked by a cougar once before. It was not a pretty sight. It had deep gashes in its flanks and the owner finally had to put it down. Had it survived the attack, it would probably have been too skittish to trust with a rider again. He hurried with the wood, wanting to get the flames going and keep any mountain lions at bay.

He dumped the wood roughly alongside where Reyes squatted outside the fire ring.

"I wish you would quit calling me '*niño*.' I am nearly sixteen, now."

"Ah, yes. You are becoming a man. Did you show my little sister how much of a man you are?"

"No! Of course not!"

"So, Maria is not good enough for you?"

Either way Andy answered, he was trapped.

"Maria is fine. It just so happens that I already have a girlfriend."

"Ah, you have a girlfriend at sixteen? Isn't that a little young?" Reyes piled the limbs in an upright triangle on the ground inside the fire ring and lit a match beneath them. The flame took off when it hit pitch. Soon the snapping wood broke the silence that had built between them.

Andy wandered over toward the horses.

"Don't think about taking off, *niñ* —young *gringo*. Reyes is still faster than you are." His laughter echoed across the mountainside.

Reyes moved to his mount and took off the saddle. He removed the halter and instructed Andy to do the same with Comet. He took his lariat and formed a loop for each horse, tying them together to the tree, giving them rope enough to be able to continue to graze the grass as far as the rope would reach.

He tossed his saddle blanket to Andy and dropped the saddle alongside the fire.

"Here, get some sleep. Tomorrow, I decide what we do."

~ * ~

Trace was up before daybreak. He left Molly dressing in their room while the children slept in. "No point in waking anyone we don't need to," he told Molly.

He went down the stairs, and into the kitchen, grabbing a cold biscuit that had fallen from the empty plate onto the table as he went past and outside to the barn.

Seth had Crazy Leg upstairs with him and the chickens were still in their coop so Trace went straight to saddle Lucky.

"Trace!" He heard Molly's alarm as he walked the horse toward the house.

Molly ran toward him.

"Maria's gone! Her blankets are spread across the floor but there's no sign of her."

"Are you sure she didn't get up early and start the chores?" He retraced, in his mind, the niches of the barn from where he had come. He hadn't seen her there. The cow was still in its stall, not in the stanchion for milking. *The chickens hadn't been let out yet, so she wouldn't be around the barnyard either,* he decided.

Molly ran to the outhouse. The door was unlatched. Maria wasn't there.

"I don't know, Molly. I have to go look for Andy. I'll watch for her, too, while I'm on my way."

"I'm going to look for her."

"What about the kids? You can't leave them alone."

"Rosie has been caring for the babies, under my supervision, for a long time. She can do it. I won't go far. If I don't find her by noontime, I'll head back. I won't leave them alone at night."

"I guess you're right. I have to go after Andy. From what I saw of the tracks this morning, he's with someone with a large horse. A horse that wears a shoe with a file mark across the metal that leaves a gap in the dirt." Although he didn't voice his next thought to Molly, Trace suspected it was Reyes. *Maybe he has Andy and Maria riding Comet double.*

He kissed Molly, quickly, and mounted Lucky.

"Be careful, Trace."

"You be careful, too. Remember, back before nightfall, with or without Maria."

"I promise."

While Trace had clear hoof prints to follow in search of Andy, Molly had no idea where to begin looking for Maria.

Molly rushed back to the house for the milk pail. With both Andy and Maria gone, she was the only one that could milk the cow and Bossy had to be milked quickly and turned out to pasture before she could leave.

The children were still asleep when Molly hitched up the buckboard and got everything ready before she went into the house to wake Rosie and inform her of her plans.

Rosie stirred slowly from her warm covers when Molly touched her shoulder.

"Rosie, wake up. I need you to do something for me," Molly said softly.

Rosie pushed her covers back, disturbing Callie where she slept in the tight crook of Rosie's knees.

"Maria's gone and I have to go after her. I'm sure she would have told us if she had planned to leave on her own. If nothing else, I have to let the sheriff know Maria's missing. Maybe he can look for her."

"Andy and Maria?" *What does the two of them being gone have to do with each other?* She knew Becky had been angry when she rode away last night, but she had not seen what went on in the barn since she and Callie hadn't entered it until after Becky left. Now, curiosity plaguing her mind, she tugged Callie up from her covers and headed downstairs with the warm cat in the bend of her arm.

"Don't wake the babies, or Seth. Let them continue to sleep and keep a good watch over them when they do wake up. Understand?"

"Yes, Ma," Rosie answered sleepily, although the realization that two people were missing from their household was quickly snapping her out of her brief grogginess.

"Trace went off on Lucky tracking Andy. I'm taking

the buckboard and I'll be back as soon as possible. Are you sure you can take care of things here?"

"Yes. I'll have Seth do the outside chores and I won't take my eyes off the babies, or him. I promise." While Rosie assured Molly of her capabilities, a thought nagged her. Could she keep her mind matched with her own body and not slip into the more comfortable habits of those of a cat?

She knew, even though Molly didn't, when she felt her body warming beside the stove, or in a sunny space, and her eyelids sagged, she would have to fight the urge to begin purring. It would be tempting to curl up in a tight ball, next to the heat of the stove or a bright sunny spot on the rug where rays of sunlight fanned across the floor. She would have to resist those temptations today.

As young as she was, she realized she would need to fight for self-control over the overwhelming urges that popped to the surface of her mind now and then.

Molly was trusting her with her younger brothers and sister. She would have to fight to be herself, Rosie, the little caretaker. She sometimes thought she had too many jobs thrust upon her, what with Molly's illness. It was times when she felt overwhelmed that it was so much easier to be like Callie. She could escape the pressures she felt when the chores became too much. For all she tried to show a tough exterior, inside Rosie was fragile. Now, she could not disappoint Molly or endanger the children.

Molly hesitated. She hated leaving Rosie in charge and putting so much responsibility on her, but, with Andy gone, she was the oldest and Molly knew she would keep the smaller kids safe if it was at all possible. She worried that someone might come up to the house and take them all.

"Keep Crazy Leg inside with you at all times," Molly suggested.

"Take care of the milk and wash the pail. I left some oatmeal in a pan. Have that for breakfast. Don't mess with the stove. If I'm not back by lunchtime, have cold biscuits and some of that cheese Mrs. Johnson gave us. I don't want you handling anything that takes a flame without me here."

"Yes, Ma."

"Once the chores are finished, stay inside. Don't let anyone know you're here. Understand?"

"Yes, Ma." Rosie felt a tug of apprehension. She had never been trusted with such an important job in her life. She'd watched over Seth when they were younger, but he usually got both of them in trouble. She didn't think he would dare do anything that would endanger the babies. She'd have to see that he didn't.

Molly grabbed one of Trace's old hats to keep the sun off her head and went out the door to the buckboard. She saw Rosie watching her from the open front door as she climbed onto the driver's seat and snapped the reins.

Rosie watched Molly move the buckboard down the lane. The sun was streaming in through the side window of the house and her mind suggested curling up on the windowsill. Her sense of reason told her she would not fit on the narrow piece of wood and she quickly shook the thought from her head.

She knew she would have to concentrate hard to stay within her own being and not slip into the mental state of a cat. Callie rubbed against her bare ankles that were exposed below her nightgown. *How lucky she is to have no human worries.* Callie simply slept, ate and played. Sometimes she chased a mouse. How Rosie yearned for a life like that!

Twelve

Tom greeted Mrs. Swartz the next morning and was leaving to have breakfast when he saw the young woman he met the evening before coming down the hall. She was dressed demurely in a dark gray flowing cotton day coat and crisp hat to match. She appeared far different than he remembered her last night. Gone was the rouge and heavy lip color. Beside her, holding her hand, walked a boy he judged to be about five years old.

"Good morning," Tom said in surprise.

"Good morning. This is my son, Elias."

Elias reached out his hand and shook Tom's with a firm grip.

"Nice to meet you, sir."

"Nice to meet you, too, Elias."

"When we met last night, I didn't give you my name. It's Shelia. Shelia Ward."

Tom looked at the woman before him with questions rising in his mind.

"Well, Shelia and Elias, I'm Thomas Jennings. I was going to go have breakfast. Perhaps your mother and you would like to join me?" He directed the question at the boy but waited for his mother to answer.

Shelia considered the offer, hesitating long enough for her son to see she didn't take an invitation lightly.

"That would be nice. But I insist we return the favor in some way."

"Perhaps you can. Or, you might already have. The information you provided me last night might be helpful to me in the future." Tom thought about the man Shelia had pointed out at the saloon.

"I understand the hotel, up the street, serves a decent breakfast. How about going there?"

"Certainly."

Elias released his mother's hand and skipped ahead, leaving the two adults to talk.

"I've thought about what you said yesterday and I've decided I should find some other line of work," Shelia told Tom.

"Having a child to raise and support can't be easy." He wondered where the boy's father was and why he wasn't in the picture, but hesitated to ask.

"Raising him by myself is difficult. I try to keep him away from the evil side of life. But, you see it all around us. The saloons—the outlaws. What's a mother to do?"

"The best you can, I guess."

"That's why we live at the boarding house. The woman that owns it, Mrs. Swartz, watches Elias at night and keeps her mouth shut. She understands you do what you have to do to feed and raise your child."

Tom nodded. He had to admire that in Shelia.

"Elias," Shelia called out, "Come back. This is the hotel."

The boy came running at her call.

Tom stood back to let Shelia go ahead and Elias moved in front of her.

The conversation soon turned to small talk with Tom showing Elias how to design shapes with the mismatched silverware on top of the tablecloth while they waited for their meal.

~ * ~

"Can I walk you back home?" Tom asked when they had finished and stood in the sunshine outside the hotel.

"No, thank you. Elias and I have to meet someone. I do appreciate your offer, though. And, thank you, so much, for breakfast."

"Thank you," Elias said as Shelia's words prompted him to remember his manners.

"You're both very welcome." It had been pleasant for Tom to share a meal with the woman and child and, although business nagged his mind, he hated to end their time together.

He watched as the two of them moved away from him down the boardwalk and turned a corner.

Somehow, he felt an emptiness like he had never experienced before and he wondered at his own emotions. He shook the feeling away and turned back to the sheriff's office.

"Well, Tom Jennings, you are a sight for sore eyes," the sheriff greeted him. "I didn't know if we'd ever see you back in this territory again."

"Business calls me back, Sheriff. Do you know about the Bennington Gang?"

The sheriff cringed. "They're a bad bunch, is about all

I can say. Hain't had no run in with them, myself, but heard tell that Rigor is locked up for killing a couple of stagecoach drivers."

"Well, I've got to escort him back to Waco to stand trial for some nasty deeds he did in Texas and I'm looking to eliminate all the trouble in doing that I can."

"Smart of ya. Some people say Rigor don't have a conscience. Things have been pretty calm around here since you and Westerman helped rid the town of Snake's gang a few years back. We sure don't need any of the Bennington gang hanging around here to cause us more trouble."

"Well, if things are as they appeared last night, I think you've got one of 'em right in you midst. I had a lady point one out to me at one of the saloons. That's what concerns me. I'm looking to make a nice peaceful ride back to Texas. I sure don't want any of his bunch trying to mess that up."

Tom gave the sheriff a description of the man he had seen the night before.

"I overheard one of the other men call him Smitty."

"I'll sure keep a watch out for him. We certainly don't want his kind around here."

"If it looks like he's fixing to ride out, have somebody keep an eye on him and anyone he might pick up, would you? I'll be heading to Albuquerque to collect Rigor and I could use any help I can get distracting any sidewinders when I come back through."

"I'll have a deputy check it out. We'll be watching." The sheriff assured him.

"Say, whatever happened to Westerman, anyway?"

"Didn't you hear? He married the Kling woman when he got back from that last ride the two of you took. Hear tell they're right happy."

"That's good. Always glad to hear something like that. Rubbing elbows with the criminal element all the time sometimes sours me on the way life plays out. Glad somebody can make a decent life for themselves."

"If I see him, I'll tell him you stopped by."

"I'll try to get back over this way and stop by their homestead sometime."

"I'm sure they'd all like that. The boy was sure glad to see Westerman come back in with his horse."

"We were pretty happy to catch up to that horse thief so he could bring him back. That was one heck of a ride and we thought sure the horse was going to end up in Mexico or shot dead."

The sheriff shook his head.

"That kid has had more trouble trying to keep someone from making off with that animal. Things seem to have settled down now, though."

"Well, I've got to get on into Albuquerque and meet up with the jail wagon."

The sheriff walked to the door to see Tom out and watched as he mounted his horse to leave. He scanned both sides of the street, looking for any sign of trouble.

"I'll get the deputy headed out looking for that fella you mentioned."

Tom reined his horse away and touched his fingers to his hat. The sheriff raised his hand and nodded his head. He called to a young boy playing in the street.

"There's a nickel for you if you find Deputy Jones and

tell him I want to talk to him," he told the boy. Immediately, the boy dropped the stick he had been using to roll a wagon rim down the street and ran on command.

The sheriff scanned the street, again, before he returned inside his stuffy office to continue his paperwork while he waited for his deputy to respond.

In the shadow of the saloon doorway a shaded figure watched Tom's back as he disappeared down the street. He bided his time until Tom was far enough down the street that he wouldn't see him follow. Then he made his way toward his horse.

The boy, intent on his errand, ran, full force, into the man.

"Here, kid! Watch what you're doing."

The man roughly grasped the boy by his shoulders and shoved him away, causing him to stumble on the edge of the boardwalk. He regained his balanced as he fell against the hitching rail. He looked up at the man in surprise.

The man moved past the boy and mounted his horse. He followed Tom at a distance. The traffic congestion on the main street of Moriarty shielded the second rider from the first. Once away from the town, the dust Tom's horse stirred barely settled before the second horse reached the same section in the road.

Thirteen

Jesus found a small cave in the mountains outside of Santa Fe to catch a few hours of sleep where he could confine Maria and keep her from escaping. By the time they stopped for the night, she was too tired to fight him and slept fitfully until he shook her awake at dawn.

"Here. I grabbed some biscuits from a plate on the homesteader's table," he tossed her one. She inspected it, knocking the dirt from its edges before she tried to eat it.

"Don't be so picky. It's food. Eat it."

"Jesus, you better take me back."

"Why? We have traveled a long way in the night. The further north we go, the less chance Reyes has of finding us."

"And you know he'll kill you when he does."

"I don't intend that to happen."

"Well, I do." The fire flared in Maria's voice. "Who do you think you are to steal me away like a farm goat or something?"

"You will see, Maria. Once we are married, you will be happy to be with Jesus."

Maria gathered saliva in her mouth and spat at him.

"You are a pig! I will never marry you."

Jesus laughed. "We go now."

He pulled Maria by her arm until she was standing on her feet.

She jerked away from him.

"Leave me alone!"

He yanked her toward the horse and dragged her up on its back. He held the reins tight, suspecting that she would attempt to get away if he wasn't careful.

She wondered where Reyes was. Why was it taking so long for him to come and find her?

Jesus walked the horse slowly down a bank to a small stream. There, he relaxed the reins and let the horse drink.

"If you want *agua*, you better drink it now. We have a long ride ahead of us."

Maria slipped off the horse and cupped her hands in the water a few feet upstream from the animal. She tried to formulate a plan of escape, knowing that Jesus could jerk the horse's reins tight and run her down before she could get far if she wasn't careful. *I will have to wait until there is a better place. Somewhere that I can hide easily.*

Jesus rode the horse carefully toward her. He reached down and grasped her arm again in a rough assist back up behind him.

~ * ~

To Trace, it appeared that Andy had purposely walked Comet in the soft dirt, at the edge of the packed ruts of the road, which led across the valley. He followed the prints the horse made, finding, now and then, another set of tracks where the other rider seemed to have tried to keep the imprints less evident by riding where the dirt was packed. He suspected they were aiming for the mountain ahead. Molly's mountain, he called it. It had supplied the rocks for the foundation of the house, food by way of the small deer that roamed there and wood for heat and cooking in the house. He studied the slope of the hill ahead and remembered his last trip up the mountainside when he had dug Molly's grave. He looked ahead and knew, precisely, in his mind's eye where it was.

Why couldn't the tribulations of life just leave them alone? It seemed to be one trial after another, for them, and it would be nice to have a quiet, happy existence without someone always getting hurt, or sick, or taken.

Molly's Mountain—now, it looked as if Andy would be there, as well. He only hoped that Andy was all right and that he would be bringing him back healthy and safe. If he ever found him again.

When he reached the trail that led up the hill, the tracks became less evident and he had to search more carefully, dismounting and remounting Lucky as he did so.

As Trace worked his way up the mountain path, he hesitated, occasionally, to look and listen intently for any indication of another human being on the hillside.

He crested the top, rode briefly along the summit then began the decline on the backside of the mountain. Within a short distance, he smelled a slight odor of smoke and found the nearly cold campfire where Reyes and Andy had spent the night.

He held his hand above the ashes, feeling for any sign of heat to determine how long the fire had been out in order to calculate how far ahead Andy and the other rider might be.

The ashes were barely warm. It appeared they had not been stirred to life for breakfast, the fuel having run out sometime in the early morning hours.

Trace moved the rocks aside and searched the ground for any sign Andy might have left.

At last, he lifted one of the stones and found a crude marking. The word "Mexico" was scratched in the dirt beneath the flat rock.

Andy had left a sign. *At least he is still alive*, Trace thought with relief.

Did Andy mean they were headed for Mexico? Maria was from Mexico. Perhaps whoever took Andy—probably Reyes—had come back and gotten Maria, as well. Perhaps they were headed for Mexico, all three of them. He had hoped he'd seen the last of that part of the world, but that was apparently not the case. His search would have to continue. He would have to travel on, to Mexico, if necessary.

Fourteen

Trace thought about Molly and wondered how her search for Maria was going. Her hunt would be futile if the horse he was tracking carried Maria as well as Andy. He hoped she was having better luck than he was. He moved Lucky along the trail, cautiously, looking for anything Andy might have left behind to lead him in the right direction.

There was a slight quiver of leaves in the brush to his right. He pulled his pistol and stopped Lucky in his tracks. The sound was subtle, then almost non-existent. Trace froze, listening intently. He had heard something. He was sure of it. Gradually he guided Lucky toward the sound, one step at a time.

As they came closer to the area where Trace thought the noise emanated, Lucky began to balk and toss his head. It was clear the horse did not want to get close to the source of the noise.

Trace kicked one foot free from the stirrup and pushed some brush aside with his boot.

"Hisssssssssss. Grrrrrrrrrrrr." A mountain lion stood on all fours to protect it's kill after they had disturbed its feeding. Blood dripped from its mouth that showed long, sharp teeth. A large jackrabbit lay ripped at its feet.

Trace jerked Lucky's reins back and to the left.

The horse sidestepped hastily, nearly buckling onto its haunches.

Trace struggled to grip the horse's belly with his thighs and dropped his hands to grasp the saddle horn.

The tawny-colored mountain lion crouched, ready to spring at the horse and rider.

"Oh, God," Trace spoke in surprise as Lucky recovered his footing and he let him lurch away and skid down part of the mountainside.

The pathway was slick, and Lucky soon worked to keep his balance in the drift of broken shale as he was caught up in a short rock slide.

Trace clung to the horse's neck, planning to ride out the downward slope that had taken them off course from the main trail. He glanced behind and saw that the big cat had stopped its pursuit when they clattered down the hillside. It stood now, pacing at the top, watching its enemy slip away. Trace only hoped Lucky could maintain the slide until he could get his footing below. It was far too dangerous to try to jump off the horse. Should Lucky fall, Trace might well be crushed beneath him.

At last, the shale thinned as the slope leveled off and Lucky was able to find his footing.

Once they were out of danger, Trace reined the horse in and sat still, allowing himself and Lucky to catch their breath. Lucky snorted through his nostrils, tossing his head and shaking his body from the mane back. Trace remained mounted, fearing that, should he dismount, the horse might bolt and run without him. He reached forward and patted the side of Lucky's neck.

"It's okay. We made it, boy." He wanted to shake himself as well, to get down and stretch his legs and readjust the crotch of his pants, but he knew he had to get the horse back up to the trail, somewhere ahead of the mountain lion, in order to look for Andy.

Trace picked his way through the brush, skirting a ravine. When he found a small, slow flowing stream, he stopped. Feeling that the horse was calm enough, now, he got off and let Lucky drink his fill. When he finished, Trace lifted each of the horse's hooves systematically to check the soft pad of flesh inside the horseshoes for stones that might bring the horse up lame.

At last, satisfied that Lucky wasn't injured, he pulled some jerky from his saddlebag and chewed on that while he studied the lay of the land and looked for the best way to get back up to the trail. While he ate, he moved around, walking to loosen the kinks in his body and modify the fit of his clothes. He bent to stretch his taut muscles.

Trace remounted and angled the horse slowly up the side of the mountain where they could intersect the path and continue down the trail that led to the next valley.

He had come this way when he first arrived in New Mexico from Texas. He remembered the trail, vaguely, and considered where it might lead. If Andy was already off the mountain, he and the other rider could be making good time across the flat land below on the other side.

When he reached the right spot up ahead, where he could look out across the valley floor, perhaps he could see them then.

He urged Lucky on down the trail, trying not to move too quickly in order to study the tracks in the hard packed earth.

Where the brush came close to the trail, having not been worn back by horses and riders he found a branch with a fresh break where someone had snapped the twig and let the broken piece dangle. It could be from riders other than the ones he sought. But, within a few feet, there was another, and another. It was no accident. There were three broken twigs close together. He rode on. He saw nothing for a few yards. Then, again, a broken twig. Another. And, yet, another. Andy was leaving him a message, he was sure.

Threes. Things happen in threes. Andy knew to fire three shots if there was danger. He was telling him he was in trouble. The kid is smart. Trace was not giving himself any credit for Andy's training.

At last, Trace reached an area where he could see clearly for miles across the open valley. Far below, dust rose from horses running on the road that crossed the valley's floor.

A sinking feeling gripped his stomach. He was sure what he saw were the horses he had been tracking. He watched as Andy sped out of his life.

Fifteen

Tom Jennings left Moriarty behind and rode toward Albuquerque. His head was full of thoughts about Shelia and Elias. *Clearly, there is no steady man in their lives. And, Trace and the Kling woman had married. I'll be darned!* He hadn't given marriage much thought in the past. He'd spent too much time on the trail of some bandit to expect a woman to sit home alone and wait for him to return.

When he finally pulled his horse up to the stockade of the prison, he was tired and hungry and in no mood to deal with surly criminals. There had been a riot there, not long ago he'd heard and he wanted no run-in with trouble. Some of New Mexico's worst criminals were behind these walls. He wasn't interested in meeting any of them he didn't have to today. He had been responsible for putting some of them in there and, if they had the opportunity, he was sure they'd be more than happy to pay him back for his trouble.

A wagon, shaped somewhat like a stagecoach, sat

alongside the wall. Solid thin sheet metal covered its sides. There was only a single barred window in the door. The opening was too small for anyone to crawl through, should they be able to remove the metal bars. It was only large enough to let a little air in for whoever was being transported. *It looks more like a portable hot box on wheels,* Tom thought. Nearby, a team of horses stood waiting to pull the heavy contraption.

A guard at the front gate checked Tom's papers and let him pass. He pointed to the warden's office.

Tom handed another guard at the door to the office the papers and was allowed to proceed.

"Evening, Warden," Tom greeted the man as he rose from his desk and pushed a chair around in front. He studied him briefly. He was a tall, husky man that appeared to have eaten too many rich meals. Although not rotund, he was massive and seemed as if he would tower over most of his charges and hired men.

"Are you the man we've been waiting for to take Bennington back to Texas?"

"Yep." Tom surrendered his orders to the warden. "It seems to be my specialty these days, escorting prisoners here or there."

"Just see that this one gets there, that's all I care. I'll be glad to have the troublemaker out of my prison. And, don't ever bring him back."

"Giving you some problems, I judge?"

"He's a flint-hearted son-of-a-bitch. He stirs up trouble everywhere he can. He's the one responsible for starting the riot last month."

Tom waited quietly as the warden sat down to study his orders.

"When you fixing to leave, in the morning?"

"No. Figure we'll head out tonight after the evening meal. Travel ought to be more comfortable in the cool of the night. Safer for me, too, I think. I don't think any of his cronies will expect that we'd move him then."

The warden nodded his agreement. "Sounds like a good plan. I'll see that Rigor gets a good belly full of food. Maybe it'll make him want to sleep most of the night."

"If he can, in that contraption."

"I've got a driver for you, Joe Mitchell, but I can't spare an extra man for a guard. You'll have to do that yourself."

"I'd hoped you'd have someone to ride shotgun. But, if you don't, I guess we'll manage. Does this Mitchell fellow carry a scattergun, anyway?"

"I'll make sure he does." The warden called to the guard at the door to see that someone passed on his message.

"You might as well have supper with me before you go."

"Thank you, warden."

Tom walked to the small window that looked out over the exercise yard of the prison. He saw guards standing around the narrow alcove between the buildings with rifles in their hands. Several prisoners milled about in the courtyard. Two sat on heavy benches and one, taller than the rest and wiry looking, leaned against a building with his arms crossed. His head was ducked so his chin touched his chest. He raised his head as if sensing he was being watched.

The warden came forward. "That's him, there, staring defiantly at the lead guard. He has never gotten along with any of them and he doesn't want to cooperate unless he's forced to. He thinks he's the boss of all the rest of the men."

Tom studied him hard. He wondered what mannerisms might clue him in on anything the man might try. But, Rigor didn't change his stance, no matter how long Tom watched him. At last, a whistle blew and the prisoners gathered into a large group. All of them, except Rigor Bennington.

"He doesn't know he's leaving," the warden said. "I figured he'd be less apt to try something if it were a surprise."

"I hear their prison talk sometimes outguesses what's in store for them."

"We try hard to keep that to a minimum. Food will be here in another hour. Do you want to catch a nap before that to help you get through the night?"

"I'd appreciate that."

"I'll have the guard take you to a cot. He'll wake you when dinner comes. I make it a practice to stay inside my office, unless there's a problem or a darned good reason to go out. The prisoners don't take too kindly to me. Seems they don't like some of the treatment they get sometimes."

Tom nodded. He wouldn't like being locked up to begin with. He'd heard some of the prisons had holes dug in the earth, that were like ovens, where a man would be put to nearly bake to death if he got out of line. Prisoner or not, he didn't figure any man deserved that kind of treatment.

Sixteen

Molly drove the buckboard to Moriarty without seeing any sign of Maria along the way. She had checked the barn when she harnessed the horses and had not found her there.

When she had led the horses to hitch them to the buckboard, she had noticed that someone had stepped in her flowerbed beneath the kitchen window and broken stalks on her precious hollyhocks. That infuriated her. The flowerbed was the one thing she did for her own pleasure. The other family members respected that. They made sure the animals and the younger children didn't trample the tender plants or larger stalks with their bright red blossoms. Everyone on the farm knew better than to mess around her flowers. She was sure it must have been whoever had taken Maria. Molly assumed, from the damage to her flowers, whoever it was, must have looked in through the kitchen window and seen Maria asleep on the living room floor. There was no sign that they had come in through the window, so they must have simply opened the front door and walked in, she decided. Maria's blankets being dragged toward the door indicated, to her, that Maria hadn't left on her own accord. She would have simply laid the blankets aside and gotten up. Once up, Molly was sure she would have folded them and left them stacked in a neat pile along with the heavy pillows.

The team had been there when Molly went to harness them. Andy had been snatched away, apparently, on Comet and Trace had Lucky. Maria would have had no means of transportation. *Unless, someone took her on their horse or had a second horse with them.*

Now, she slowly pulled the buckboard alongside the boardwalk and tied the team to the rail outside the sheriff's office. She went inside.

"Why, howdy, Miz Kling, uh, Miz Westerman," the sheriff greeted her.

"Sheriff." Molly noticed the man appeared groggy, as if he had been napping. His hair was astray and his face wore more wrinkles than she remembered seeing in the dark last night.

"What brings you into town?" The sheriff filled a coffee pot with cold water from a pitcher as he waited for her answer.

"We've had a girl staying with us. You know, the one you saw at the house last night."

"Yes, the Mexican girl." He recalled seeing the family at their house before the posse had given up searching for the horse thief.

"That's right, her name's Maria. Anyway, Andy went missing last night after you were there. When we got up this morning, before daybreak for Trace to go looking for him, she was gone, too."

The sheriff raised his eyebrows. His mind seemed too

fogged with sleep to totally comprehend the situation.

"Well, if they're both gone..."

"I don't think they ran off together," Molly said, immediately picking up on his insinuation. Trace went after Andy. He's gone on his horse and, unless Maria was riding double with him, it didn't appear she went when Andy did. Maria had laid down in the living room. Then, when we got up, her blankets were all in disarray and dragged toward the front door. I think someone else took her."

"Possible, I guess. But, why?"

"I don't know. When Trace and Andy found her out at the back of our pasture and brought her into the house, she'd been pretty beat up. She never talked about what happened. I don't even know if she remembers."

"So, you think, maybe, whoever did that to her, came back and got her?"

"Maybe. I really don't think she'd go off on her own. Look, I've left the kids alone at the house. I have to get back. Can you have someone search for her?"

"Sure, I'll get one of my deputies to ride on over toward Albuquerque. I'll send one on up toward Santa Fe, too. If she didn't head back to Mexico, those two towns would be my guess. By the way, that friend of Trace's was in here this morning. The Texas Ranger you brought in to Doc Landry that had gotten shot in the back."

"Oh, you mean Tom?"

"Yes. Tom Jennings. He's headed over Albuquerque way. If he shows back up, I'll ask him to keep a watch out for her, too."

"Thank you, Sheriff. I know Maria's not really our

responsibility but, she was supposed to be safe in our home. If she wasn't, then, I feel responsible, whether I am or not."

"You go on home, Mrs. Westerman. Let me take care of it."

"I guess I should." Molly thought about the babies and prayed Rosie was keeping them safe.

She returned to the buckboard and moved it down the street where she could turn it around and head back for the homestead. She planned to be there before dark, as she had promised Trace and Rosie.

~ * ~

Unbeknownst to Molly, Maria and Jesus had not covered much distance on their ride toward Santa Fe. Once Jesus found the cave and they had slept the night, Maria did everything she could to slow him down.

When they stopped a short distance from where Jesus had watered the horse, to rest the animal that was barely strong enough to be carrying one rider, much less two, Maria found a boulder to hide behind and slipped away.

When she heard Jesus approach, she called out, "Don't come any closer. Give me a minute."

Jesus, suspecting that she was taking care of bodily necessities, stepped back and let her have her privacy.

He inspected the horse and his gear and checked the animal's hooves, lifting its legs one by one, to inspect the soft pad inside the metal shoe for rocks or thorns. It was more a way to occupy his time, than a necessity.

"*Pressa!*" He finally called to her. "Hurry up. What is taking you so long?"

He gave her a few more minutes.

"Get out here, now!"

When she didn't respond, Jesus moved angrily toward the rock.

"All right, *señorita*, I am coming back there," he warned so she could answer him and save herself embarrassment.

No answer returned.

Jesus made his way through the brush and around the large boulder.

"Maria! Where are you, Maria?"

He looked beyond the boulder to the next, and the next, and ran from one to the other. There was no sign of the girl.

"*Mierda!*" Jesus blurted out in disgust. *What is wrong with that girl? She could die out here alone. Doesn't she know that?*

He ran back to the horse and mounted, planning to search for her until he found her, or was forced to give up hope.

~ * ~

Trace moved off the mountain and pushed Lucky into a run as soon as the ground was smooth enough to travel at a faster speed.

The other horses had a big lead on him and he questioned whether he could catch them or not. Where they had been moving straight across the valley, it now appeared the dust trail was drifting slightly from the north. Were they doubling back toward Santa Fe? If he could cut straight across, he might intercept them before they got away. But, there were too many obstructions to do that. He would have to follow the same path they had until he reached the crossroad that led from west to east and connected to another trail north toward Estancia, Moriarty and the homestead.

He had been trailing Andy nearly all day, now, and the ride was wearing on him. He saw a farmhouse in the distance and wondered if Molly had gotten back to their house with Maria. It seemed to him that he, and the horses ahead, was riding in a big circle. If they were headed back to the homestead, he only hoped he could close the distance between himself and them.

He didn't know if Rosie was still at the house with the kids alone or if Molly had returned. Either way, there could be trouble. Rosie would be unprotected. Even with Molly there and her rifle close by, whoever was with Andy might well get the upper hand on Molly if they were headed back to the house and got there before he did.

Trace worried about his family. *It seemed if they didn't have bad luck, they had no luck at all.*

~ * ~

Tom finished his meal with the warden with dusk falling to conceal their start back toward Moriarty with the jail wagon and get past the town under cover of darkness. He hoped to be well on his way through New Mexico by daylight the next morning. He had no plans to go into town, avoiding it on a side trail that ran between the town and the homesteader's spread. The thought crossed his mind to stop and see if Trace would ride shotgun with him into Texas. He'd decide that when he got closer to the homestead.

For now, he watched two surly guards lead Rigor Bennington to his carriage. His hands were tied behind his back. His feet were shackled with a short length of chain between large metal rings around his ankles. A flour sack had been pulled over his head. There was a guard on each side, grasping his upper arms and escorting him to the waiting wagon. When they reached the door, one of the guards drew a knife and cut the rope that bound his hands.

Tom saw the prisoner reach forward and touch the steel sides of the door's frame. A guard prodded him and he climbed aboard, still blinded by the flour sack. When he was inside the cage, the guard slammed the door shut and the second guard slipped a padlock through the loop on a hasp and locked it.

The warden walked up behind Tom. He handed him a second key to the rolling prison. It was attached to a small key ring that also held a key to ankle shackles as well and some that fit nothing Tom was in charge of at the time.

"Be cautious with that one. He can get real mean."

Tom nodded. He intended to be careful.

~ * ~

Maria, hiding far back in a stony canyon behind large boulders, had watched Jesus as he hunted for her. She waited until he wandered on in the other direction, then she picked her way around the rocks, making sure not to expose herself.

She made her way back to the trail that led toward Moriarty and the link to Albuquerque. As the hours dragged on, she walked, energetically at first. Then, as her strength began to dwindle, she found herself forcing one foot ahead of the other. All the while, she listened intently for the sound of a horse and rider, fearing that Jesus would figure out the way she had come and find her.

The day became an eternity. Without water or food, Maria felt herself fading fast. Her fight for survival became laborious.

I have to keep going, she urged herself on. She reasoned, if she followed the road toward Moriarty she would eventually come to the town. She could go on to the homestead from there.

Perhaps I should give up on the idea of Reyes saving me and find a way back home to Mexico on my own. She had grown fond of the family that had so kindly taken her in. Yet, a wave of homesickness washed over her as she thought about her own family in Mexico. She missed her mother and father. She missed her friends and the gaiety of the *fiestas*.

She recalled the night Jesus had carted her away from Reyes' engagement party and wondered how much her family and friends missed her. She tried to occupy her mind with pleasant thoughts, and shook the sadness away, as the heat of the afternoon became smothering and she stumbled along the road. She gathered the hem of her heavy skirt and lifted it up over one arm so that what little breeze was available blew across her knees and thighs.

She trudged along, struggling to keep moving in the right direction and not give up along the way. She stopped to rest, moving away from the open road into the concealment of tall bushes. She slept the early evening away and, when she awoke, made her way back to the road and, getting her bearings once more by the bright stars, headed again for Moriarty.

~ * ~

Tom was feeling almost too sure of himself. So far, the

ride from the prison had been uneventful. Traveling late in the evening and through the night looked like the answer to his problems. They had skirted Moriarty successfully. The drive was going so well he decided not to disturb the Westerman family and go on to Waco without Trace.

Already it was nearing midnight and there had been no trouble with Rigor Bennington. He had seemed to sleep without a problem and Joe Mitchell had been able to keep the horses at a steady pace along the road.

The moon was high, now, illuminating the roadway and keeping the horses on track.

The ride was almost becoming boring for Tom. He listened to the heavy creaking sound the wagon made as its wheels missed the ruts and rode the crest between them before dropping back down into the tracks left by other wagons before it.

To break the boredom, Tom rode behind the wagon for a while, then raced ahead to lead the way again.

He hoped his sudden bursts of surprise would keep Joe awake and guiding the horses properly.

For now, he rode behind watching the outline of the coach lumber back and forth in the dim light.

Joe slowed the team.

Tom spurred his horse ahead.

"What's wrong?"

"I thought I saw something up ahead. It was just a quick movement. Like someone dashing into the brush."

Tom pulled his gun and held it in the air.

"Get you're shotgun. I don't intend on anybody taking our prisoner."

"What's goin' on?" Rigor's sleepy voice came from

inside the wagon.

Tom ignored him. *Damn, now he's awake and we'll have to deal with him besides whoever else is out here.*

"Keep an eye on the prisoner. I'll ride up ahead and see what I can find." Tom moved his horse forward, walking him cautiously in the direction Joe pointed.

All was quiet. *You could hear a mouse squeak*, Tom thought. He listened for a pistol to cock, a horse to whinny, or any sound, or movement, out of the ordinary.

The whirr of a grouse in the underbrush startled his horse and Tom calmed him.

A twig snapped beside him. He spun his horse around, ready to fend off an attacker.

No one was there.

He dismounted, gun still in hand, and worked his way around the rear of his horse. The moonlight was not bright enough for him to see plainly beneath the brush. He pushed a limb aside with his arm and crept slowly toward the noise.

Cowered down into a burrow of brush was a girl. She cringed as he moved toward her.

"What are you doing out here, all alone, on the trail? You are alone, aren't you?"

Maria shook her head "yes" but in the dim light, Tom could not see her movement.

"I asked if you were alone."

"*Sí*." Her eyes were large with fear and she tried to scoot further away from the man. She wrapped her arms around her knees becoming what she hoped would be a difficult lump to move.

"Who are you, *señor*?"

"I'm a lawman. If you've got anyone else with you, you better say so now. Otherwise, I'm going to have to tie you up and search this whole area."

"No. Don't tie me up, please. There's no one else. How can I believe you are the law?"

Tom reached inside his vest pocket and fished his badge out with his fingers. He unpinned it and handed it to Maria. He waited while she studied the circle with a five-pointed star inside.

She looked up at him and handed the badge back.

"Do you have water?"

Tom studied her in the dim light. She appeared close to exhaustion and in need of rescue. He reached for the canteen where its strap hung across his saddle horn and dropped it alongside the girl.

She greedily downed several sips.

He reached over and took it from her before she drank too much.

"You've been out here awhile?"

"Since early morning. I've been walking and hiding from a coyote that took me from my home. I think I finally got away from him." The level of Maria's voice dwindled. *How much should I tell this man—gringo lawman or not?*

"Well, I don't know what else to do with you, except take you with us. I don't have time to stop and find someone to leave you with."

A sense of relief swept over Maria. *Regardless where they were headed, it had to be better than being on the trail alone without food or water. Surely, this gringo with his lawman badge can protect me from Jesus.*

"I'm not going to hurt you." Tom reached his right hand out to her still holding his pistol in his left. If she wasn't alone, he was not about to get jumped by someone else hiding in the brush.

Finally, Maria reached up and took his hand, letting him lead her out of the brush and back alongside the wagon.

"Thank you for helping me. My name is Maria. If you could drop me at the next *casa* or *ciudad*, I think it might be the one they call Moriarty, I would be very grateful."

"I can't guarantee that. We're on the east side of town. We don't have time to take you back there. We may have to wait until after we get to Waco to decide what to do with you."

"Where is this Waco?"

"It's a long ways from here. But, we'll see what turns up in the meantime."

They approached the waiting wagon.

"Well, what we got here?" Joe asked Tom when he saw he was not alone.

"Guess she's what you saw duck into the brush."

"Thank God! I'm not wanting to deal with some vicious bandit, or one of Bennington's gang, here."

"Have you seen anyone else along the road?" Tom questioned Maria.

She shook her head.

"No."

"She can ride with me," Rigor offered with an uproarious laugh.

Maria shuddered.

The contraption they were pulling didn't look like

anything she wanted to get into, especially with the evil sounding man inside.

"Shut up, Rigor," Tom said.

Noting her apprehension, Tom told her, "I'm a Texas Ranger. I showed you my badge. Joe, up there, is driving a prisoner back to Waco for me. No need for you to worry. I won't make you ride with him and he can't get out of his cage."

"Make room up there for her, Joe, we can't leave her out here in the middle of nowhere."

When Maria situated herself next to Joe he asked, "You know how to use one of these things?" He handed her the shotgun.

"No. I've shot a *pistola* and a rifle, but not a gun this big."

"Recon' you'll learn fast if we get stopped by Rigor's gang."

Tom mounted his horse. "Let's get this thing rolling again. We're quite a ways from civilization, yet, and I don't want to dally any longer than we have to."

Joe cracked the whip across the horses' rumps and the heavy carriage began to creak as the wheels rolled slowly again.

~ * ~

Molly returned to the homestead at dusk.

She was disappointed that she was coming back empty-handed. Maria had been nowhere to be found and she only hoped Trace had had more luck than she and returned with Andy.

She saw no sign of their horses when she approached the corral.

"I did everything like you said, Ma," Rosie assured her when she entered the house tired and hungry.

Molly reached down and picked Jacob up from the floor.

"Have you been a good boy for Rosie?" Molly asked as she kissed the baby on his head.

Jacob squirmed, stretching to get back down where he could move about on his own.

Emmy tugged at Molly's skirts. She released Jacob and pulled Emmy into her arms.

"Little Mr. Independence," Molly said to Jacob as he quickly pushed himself up to take a few clumsy steps while holding onto a kitchen chair on his way over to investigate Callie's ears.

"And how about you, Emmy?"

Emmy chattered back.

"No Trace or Andy?" Molly asked Rosie.

"No. Seth thought he saw someone coming early in the afternoon but it was only a dust devil stirring up the dirt."

Molly frowned. She had hoped they would beat her home. Now, she wondered when, or if, they would ever get back.

"They will come home, won't they, Ma?"

"If there's any way at all, Rosie."

"What about Maria? Will she come back?"

"I certainly wish I had your extra sense you had after the wagon accident to tell. I just don't know."

"I wish my knowing what was going to happen in the future hadn't gone away with the headaches."

"Your clairvoyance," Molly told her. When Rosie gave her a questioning look, Molly explained, "I looked it up, and studied it some, when I had text books shipped for teaching at the school this fall. The book said some people have it all their lives. Others, like you, only see things sporadically or temporarily."

"I'd give anything to know what's happening now. I know Maria isn't family, but I miss her." She thought about the night she had taunted her in the barn, and regretted it. She didn't know what came over her, sometimes, when she acted like, no—became—a cat. It didn't matter whether it was a small one like Callie, or a big one, which was threatening, like the one she had become in the barn and scared Maria, her own actions perplexed her. She hoped that wasn't why Maria left.

Molly moved to the front door and walked out onto the porch still carrying Emmy in her arms. Although the child was nearly two years older than Jacob, she didn't weigh much more and it was as easy for Molly to carry her as it was the baby.

They looked off into the dimly moonlit night, Molly willing to see Trace or Andy, or both.

Emmy snuggled against her mother's chest.

"You're all tuckered out, aren't you? We better get you two ready for bed. Where's Seth, Rosie?"

"He was right here. Seth," Rosie called out to her little brother.

Molly felt a second's start of panic. She feared he had wandered off, or that someone might have taken him, too. She listened intently for his answer.

"I'm right here. I was closing up the chickens."

"Well, get in here then. You gave us a scare," Rosie said, sounding more like his mother than his sister.

Molly reached out and touched Seth's shoulder as he entered the front doorway.

"Have you stayed out of trouble today?"

"Yes, Ma."

Seth flipped the silver *concho*, Crazy Leg had found, between his fingers and into his clamped fist. Crazy Leg bumped his nose against Seth's palm, sniffing to see if there was a treat there for him.

She knew he was beginning to feel he was too old for too much attention, so she resisted the urge to hug him tight as he passed by her. Instead, she noted the dog's actions.

"What have you got there?"

Reluctantly, Seth stretched his hand out and showed her the piece of metal.

"Where'd you get that?" Molly felt a stab of fear in her mind.

"Crazy Leg had it. I don't know where he got it. He brought it into the house and dropped it on the floor last night. I took it from him."

"Fine. It is good you kept it away from the babies."

Molly remembered seeing similar decorations before. They were *conchos* used by the likes of Reyes Espiañata. She remembered him well and, now, here was proof, to her, that he had been the one to take Andy.

She worried more about Andy and Trace knowing the history of their previous run ins with the man. She had thought they had seen the last of him. Why was he back to torment them further?

"You can go on to bed, Seth," she tried to keep her voice calm and handed the metal piece back to the child.

She slipped the sleepy Emmy into the cradle of her arms and went to put the other children to bed for the night.

She would wait up a bit for Trace and Andy by herself, but it was beginning to look like that was going to be useless. Wherever they were, they'd probably bed down by some campfire somewhere until morning. She only hoped they would return soon. The worry about Reyes chased memories of him around in her brain.

~ * ~

Tom was becoming complacent when the Bennington gang hit.

It wasn't one man, but three, that struck. They came riding out of the shadows at the crossroads where Joe would turn the wagon south to pull into a stage stop a few miles past Moriarty.

Previously, Tom had thought they had made it safely to their destination for a rest break.

The town was a few flickering bonfires and blinking lanterns far off to their left. He could smell the odor of burning wood and kerosene in the air as the mild stench drifted from the town on the night breeze.

"Whoa up there, old man," the voice boomed out of the shadows as the wagon turned slowly onto the road that lead toward the stage stop and a brief rest.

Guns drawn and ready to fire, three men rode close alongside the metal wagon.

Maria clutched the shotgun tight.

"Don't do it. I don't take to shooting a woman, but I will if I have to," one man called up to Maria.

"What kind of contraption is this?" Tom overheard a

second one ask another.

"Rigor? You in there?" The third voice called out as if wondering if they had been fooled about where they would find their leader.

"Where the hell else do you think I'd be, Smitty?" Rigor's voice echoed back from the inside of the cage. "What took you so long?"

"We had to wait until the three of us could get together. We sure didn't want to go up against the law without enough of us to get the job done."

"Get this door open and let me out."

"You, on the horse. Unlock the door."

"Don't have a key." Tom answered back.

"You gotta have a key. You gotta be able to let him out now and then. Ride on over there, Jeb, and shake that key out of him," the man called Smitty said.

Maria watched for an opportunity to use the shotgun.

"Take that gun from the girl, old man. Toss it down here," Smitty ordered.

Joe did as he was told. Reluctantly, Maria gave up the weapon and Joe tossed it to the man that appeared to be in charge.

"Now, the two of you get down and get over by your friend, here."

"Best do as he says," Tom suggested.

Joe got to the ground and reached up to help Maria.

The second man dismounted and walked up to Tom.

"Get off your horse."

Tom obeyed.

The man felt in Tom's vest side pocket for the key.

Tom held himself still in an attempt not to give the man

an excuse to fire his pistol. He realized he was suddenly reliving the time he was shot in the back and nearly died. The piece of lead Doc Landry had cut out of his back hung, now, on his watch fob that looped below the vest pocket holding the key.

He distracted himself from the man's urgent digging for the key by considering the fact that the watch was in the right vest pocket. There he could always lift the watch to check the time while he kept his left hand free to reach for his pearl-handled pistol, if necessary. He felt a wave of heat wash over him as the memory of the pain, from the bullet, flooded into his mind. He fought the sensation to keep from breaking into a cold sweat.

"What's takin' so long, Smitty?" Rigor demanded.

"Knew you were lyin' to us," Jeb said as he pulled the small key ring out of Tom's vest pocket. "Here it is Smitty," he lightly tossed it to the other man.

"Damn, take it easy. You make me miss it and we could be out here all night trying to find it in the brush and dirt. What's the matter with you, Jeb?"

"He loses that key, and he'll have me to deal with when I finally get out of here," Rigor said from where his hands grasped the bars on his window and his nose stuck through the spacing between two bars.

"Now, you get over here by your friends."

Tom complied.

"That man is in Texas Ranger custody. You set him free and there's going to be a whole slew of Rangers on your tail," Tom said.

Rigor laughed.

"What difference does that make? You're taking me to

hang or rot in some other stinkin' hole in Texas. I might as well enjoy what fresh air I can in the meantime. Maybe, if I'm lucky, they'll never find me."

Rigor clung to the window bars while his gang member unlocked the door.

"Get these damn shackles off me, too."

The man fingered through the small key ring until he found one that would fit the lock on the leg irons.

Rigor stepped from the coach.

"Get the girl," he ordered. "We're taking her with us."

"We only brought one extra horse. That's for you," Smitty protested.

Rigor sized Maria up. "She don't weigh much. She won't slow us down. Put her up in front of you. And, watch her."

Tom contained himself. He figured, at this point, anything he said, or did, would only endanger Maria, or Joe, more. He'd have to figure some way of handling the situation later.

Maria turned and scampered back up to the box of the wagon.

"Here! You get back down here! Jeb, you pull her down," Rigor ordered.

"Let me," the third man, who had been quietly watching the scene play out from one good eye said. He wore a black patch across his other eye and when he opened his mouth to smile in the moonlight a scraggy cavern of broken teeth showed. He sounded too gleeful about getting his hands on Maria to suit Tom.

Tom watched Maria as Rigor's crony dragged her from her perch atop the wagon. She clung tightly to the cold metal bar that ran around the seat that was designed to keep the driver and his companions from sliding off.

"Come on," the man tugged at her. She kicked at him and clipped him in the chin. He fell to the ground. He had already pulled her past the edge of the seat. Maria was forced to cling to the seat rim and try to pull herself back up onto the top, or lose her grip and fall to the earth beside him.

The man cursed, got to his feet, and came back to grab her ankles and pull her the rest of the way off the wagon.

Tom fought the urge to step in. Smitty must have sensed he was about to move. Tom heard him click the hammer back on his pistol.

Maria continued to fight, even though the man now had his arms wrapped tight around her waist and was dragging her to his horse. She flailed her arms and legs as hard as she could. She aimed to connect with another blow of her fists to his head before he could shove her up onto the horse.

Rigor mounted the horse that had been led behind one of the other riders. He took the reins and looked back at Tom.

"Guess I won't be stayin' in your accommodations any longer."

He took the gun belt, Smitty handed him and cinched it around his middle. He adjusted it and ran his hand around the leather belt like someone appreciating a new set of clothes.

"Damn, it feels good to have my guns back."

Joe moved to reach toward a rack that held a rifle. Tom was close enough to him now his gaze connected with the older man's eyes and he, silently, sent the message to him that now was not the time.

The time would come. Tom was sure. He vowed, to himself, he would hunt the gang down if he had to track them all the way to uninhabited territory.

Seventeen

When Rigor and his gang rode off into the night, Tom felt lucky to still have his horse and his gun. No one was dead and he considered that a blessing. He and Joe were left with an empty wagon. They had to contend with an escaped prisoner and a lost passenger.

"You drive on back to Moriarty. Tell the sheriff there what happened. Warn him to be on the look out for Rigor and see if he can form a posse to meet up with me. I'll trail 'em as close as I can."

"How's the posse going to find you?"

"Have 'em head this way and look for tracks. Those of my horse and four other horses."

"Right!" Joe snapped the whip over the team's head, letting it pop close behind the two lead animals. The wagon jerked and wobbled along the rutted road as he hurried to turn it and reverse his trip to Moriarty.

~ * ~

Trace, still following Andy and his captor, realized he was being led around in one big circle. They were traveling toward home but getting no closer as they went.

What is this guy doing? Trace wondered.

At last, he saw a small blaze of a campfire off to his right. He walked his horse quietly, then slid off the saddle and crept forward for a better look. When he was close enough, he saw Andy sitting alone, alongside the blaze. He seemed uncomfortable and kept glancing around the area nervously.

Why is he alone, here, now? He's near enough to the homestead he could find his way home with no problem. Comet could take him there easily, if he just gave the horse its head.

Trace heard the sound of a gun cocking behind his right ear.

"You move, *gringo*, and you are dead."

It's a trap. I should have known.

"Stand up. Move on into the firelight."

"Andy, you all right?" Trace asked as he approached.

Andy stood up.

"Yes."

"I told him long ago, I don't hurt *niño*s," Reyes told Trace.

"Then why do you keep causing us trouble?"

"It is not always I that causes the trouble. A stupid *vaquero* that used to ride with me created the problem with the horse when you chased us to the *Rio Grande*. I was willing to win the horse, or buy him, fair and square."

"If you didn't have anything to do with him stealing Comet, then why are you back, again, stealing the horse and our boy?"

"The same stupid *vaquero* that stole the horse, I think stole my little sister, Maria."

Trace looked at Andy.

"I already told Pa you were looking for Maria," Andy told Reyes. "I told Reyes we'd gladly let him take her, but he thought you'd kill him for taking Comet the last time." Andy explained to Trace.

Trace sensed Reyes still held his six-shooter on him.

"Well, now, he has a bigger problem. Maria's gone from our house, too. It looks like someone took her from there."

"Damn, Jesus!" Reyes blurted.

"Sit down, *gringo*. We rest for the night. Jesus has a little lazy in him. If I know him, he'll not travel on for very many hours."

Trace sat down next to Andy.

Andy pulled a stick from the fire that had some cooked rabbit flesh dangling from its tip. He handed it to Trace.

"I will have my eye and my gun on you all night, *gringo*, so you better not try anything."

Reyes leaned against his saddle and watched Trace and Andy at the fire.

Trace rose.

"Where you going, *gringo*?"

"Figure, if we're staying here tonight, I better unsaddle my horse."

Andy had Comet tied nearby and he looked to see that he was still secure.

"You let the *niño* do it. I think I can trust him not to run off when I could shoot you if he does."

He looked at Andy to see that the message was clearly understood.

Andy nodded. He wouldn't do anything stupid that would put Trace in any more danger.

~ * ~

It was morning before the posse caught up with Tom. He had followed the bandits up one trail and then another and, finally, approached a small box canyon hidden by heavy overgrowth.

He was familiar with the terrain from past trips into the deserted area.

He was tired. He appeared beyond exhaustion when the sheriff pulled his men up alongside Tom's horse and stopped.

The sheriff sized him up, noting that he was at less than his best.

"Tom," he greeted him. "We came as fast as we could when Mitchell got the jail wagon into town."

"Thanks, Sheriff. I figured Joe would fill you in."

"Yep. He did. I can't say as how I like it. If Rigor's got that girl with him and three extra gun hands I don't see how we're goin' to get her out without getting her hurt in the process."

"Me, either. But, we gotta try. I knew I didn't dare let them get too far ahead of me or we'd never catch up with them again."

The sheriff studied the landscape around him.

"Figure as early in the morning as it is, maybe we can catch them off guard. Wish we knew if they had any whiskey with them. If they were up drinking all night, they might be too hung over to realize we're here until it's too late."

Tom thought of the possibilities. If there had been drinking going on, it didn't bode well for Maria.

"What's up in this canyon, you got any idea?" The

sheriff asked Tom.

"Last time I was up this way, there was an old shanty there. Some homesteader had given up after picking land with the wrong lay to it, I figured."

"Looks like there's no way out the back."

"That's right. I found a herd of small horses up here once, not much bigger than milk goats. Littlest things you ever did see. Try as they might, they couldn't get out the back and had to run right past me to get away."

The sheriff stuck his finger in his mouth to wet it, then raised it into the air, checking for wind direction. The posse waited for him to make his plan.

The morning was calm. What little breeze there was waft gently in the right direction to suit him.

"So, if we work our way quietly around behind, they'll have to come out this way?" The sheriff was plotting a trap.

"Right."

"So, let's do that. I'll leave one of my men here and when we're in position he can light a blaze in this brush. When they smell smoke, they'll run out and, once they see the flames, they'll run right back into our hands."

Tom nodded. It was as good a plan as any he'd come up with. He was too tired to think of anything better.

"Watson, you stay behind. Count to five hundred, if you can do that. Then light the brush a fire. Not a big blaze, mind you, just enough so they think they have to run."

The deputy tipped his hat and slid off his horse.

"The rest of you, come with me," the sheriff ordered.

~ * ~

Jesus had followed Maria, not catching up until he saw the lumbering wagon stop to pick her up along the road.

His body had strongly required sleep but he knew if he didn't stay close behind, Maria would be lost to him forever.

He had hid in the underbrush when the outlaws stopped the wagon. He saw them ride off with Maria. The wagon and the *gringo* on horseback had parted company. Thinking the rider was following the men that took Maria, he forced himself to stay awake and follow, keeping out of sight, and far enough behind, that the rider would not hear his horse behind him.

When the posse arrived, Jesus determined his chance of getting Maria back was useless. He quietly walked his horse back down the trail toward the crossroad to Santa Fe.

As much as he loved Maria, no woman was worth the enormous risk he would have to take to get her back. He would bide his time. Unless Reyes found Maria, there was no proof that he had been the one to take her from Mexico. If he did find her, he knew Reyes would believe her over him. Perhaps he would go back, across the border, and let these *gringos* deal with Maria's current situation. He might still live to capture his love another day. Besides, he was getting sleepy, hungry and thirsty. He knew there was *tequila* in Santa Fe—and, perhaps, the possibility of sleep before he got there.

Eighteen

Molly waited anxiously for Andy and Trace to return. She thought about Maria and wondered if there was more she could have done to help find the girl.

It was dark, now, and she dared not leave the children alone. It would be far too dangerous. Despite her desire to see that Maria was safe, she had to live with her priorities.

She gazed out the front window, once more, before giving up for the night and checking the children in their beds to see that they were sleeping safely.

She returned to drop the latch across the front door before she retired.

~ * ~

The next morning, Maria, long awake and prepared to defend herself should any of the men come near her, smelled smoke before the men awoke. She had managed to wear the ropes apart, that had been tying her hands together, and quickly untied her ankles.

She crept silently toward the small hole that served as a window in the old cabin and looked outside. A slight crackling noise came to her ears and she searched the terrain until she saw the lick of a flame creeping up the brush at the outlet of the canyon.

Without sounding an alarm, she moved to let herself out the door opening where one hinge held the dilapidated door to its frame.

Let these banditos roast like the pigs they are for all I care. She moved silently around to the back of the shack and looked for an escape route around the fire.

"Over here, Maria," Tom called in a quiet tone. He motioned with his hand for her to come quickly to him.

Surprised to see the lawman hiding behind the house, Maria did as she was told.

"We're safe here. The wind is still enough the fire will fall back and burn itself out," Tom assured her.

"There's only enough breeze to stir up smoke and flush 'em out here," the sheriff added.

Tom hoped the sheriff was right. He had no plan to stay around if the fire didn't behave as the sheriff said. Already the horses were prancing and anxious to be turned loose to run away from the flames.

Suddenly, there was a loud uproar in the shack. The men came tumbling out, fighting each other to be the first to escape.

"What the hell did you do with the horses," Rigor asked Jeb as he stumbled around still trying to get his bearings.

"Tied 'em right here behind the building. They're gone now though."

"Well, I can see that!"

"Maybe they broke loose when they first smelled the smoke," Smitty suggested.

"How the hell are we supposed to get out of here,

now?" The man with the eye patch asked.

Rigor and the men sprinted for the back of the canyon.

"That's far enough," the sheriff called out as he rose above the rock he had been hiding behind. His deputies and Tom stood up, too, with their guns drawn.

"You'd a left the girl behind in there to die, wouldn't ya?" The sheriff stared at Rigor.

Rigor stared back at him.

Maria stood up from her shelter alongside Tom.

Even as she did, she could see the flames had died down and only pitchy-smelling skeletons of dry brush remained where she had seen an inferno before.

"You worthless pigs! You are lucky you are not in Mexico. You are lucky the *gringos* will deal with you, instead of my family."

"*Señor* Tom. Can we go now?" Maria had had enough of the activities across the border. She was ready to go home and stay there for awhile.

"As soon as we can get this bunch tied and onto horses, we'll head for Moriarty," the sheriff told her. "Tom can take the whole lot of them on to Texas from there in the jail wagon. I don't think there'll be anyone else wanting to break any of them out."

Tom helped Maria up onto his horse behind him while the posse got Rigor's gang mounted.

They began the trek back to Moriarty and the waiting wagon.

~ * ~

It was midmorning when Molly heard riders coming in.

"Hurry! Get into the house. Now!" Molly called to the children to drop their chores and take safety where she could protect them.

"Quickly," she said as she grasped her rifle and pulled it from its rack above the fireplace mantle.

"Who is it, Ma?" Seth asked.

"I don't know, yet. But, whoever it is, you stay in here until I tell you it's safe to go out."

Rosie clutched the babies close to her while Molly took up her position behind the front door where she could look out the window alongside that opened out onto the porch. She raised the curtain carefully with the end of the rifle barrel.

She knew it was more than one horse from the sound of the hooves. They were riding fast and the sound increased as they drew nearer to the house.

Soon she saw the glint of light from silver *conchos* on the one rider's tack and hat.

A *sombrero*, she thought, keeping the words to herself so she wouldn't frighten the children worse. As the riders drew closer, she recognized Reyes. But, Trace and Andy rode alongside him, their horses minimized by the size of the strong, black steed Reyes sat.

She lowered her gun, but kept it ready in case Trace and Andy needed her help. Maybe Reyes was more than just riding with them. Maybe he was forcing them to bring him back to the house.

The three pulled up to the hitching rail in front of the house and dismounted. Trace hurried to the door while Andy tied Lucky and Comet.

Molly burst the door open and fell into his arms.

"Thank God, you're back. And, Andy?"

"He's fine. That's Reyes Espiañita out there with him.

He's the one that dragged him away."

Molly looked up at Trace with a puzzled expression across her face.

"I recognized him from when he and his *vaqueros* were in Moriarty that time. But what is he doing with you?"

"I think we've got things worked out," Trace assured her. "Reyes is Maria's brother. He thought we were holding Maria against her will. Guess we can't blame him for what he did, in that case."

Andy came through the door and Reyes stood behind him outside on the porch.

The handsome man removed his black *sombrero* and held it in his hands.

"We spent the night camped along the trail. Reyes is convinced one of his former *vaqueros* kidnapped Maria in Mexico and brought her here. I think, maybe, he's the one that took her away from here, too. Did you find out where she went?"

"No. I talked to the sheriff and he was sending deputies to look for her, but what good is one or two deputies going to do?"

"They'd have to get awfully lucky."

Molly released Trace and hugged Andy, brushing his hair from his eyes with her hand.

"Thank God you're all right." She looked over his head straight at the man standing on her porch.

"I apologize, *Señora*. We have had reasons to not trust each other, your men and me. Now, I think those reasons were mostly caused by Jesus."

Molly studied him as he tucked his *sombrero* under one arm and ran his fingers through his thick black hair.

She gave him a look that let him know she only believed part of what he said.

"Maria is not here. I did what I could, but there was no way I could leave my children any longer and go after her any further than I did."

"I thank you for your efforts, *Señora.* Now, I must see if I can find her. Jesus, I am sure, will go where there is plenty of *tequila* and *frijoles.*"

"I'm going to ride along with Reyes, at least as far as Moriarty. Andy can stay behind with you. I don't want him in the middle of something, if it comes to shooting."

Andy gave Trace a disappointed look.

"You heard, Andy. This could be too dangerous for you."

"You're *padre* is right, *niño.* I may have to kill Jesus to get Maria back. That is no place for you."

Molly didn't even try to suggest they wait and have something to eat. She knew every minute would count in finding Maria. She would not hinder that.

Trace kissed her quickly. Reyes replaced his *sombrero* and touched his fingertips to its brim.

Molly noticed one *concho* was missing from its band.

"*Muchos gracias, Señora.* Thank you for helping my little sister."

Trace turned to follow Reyes.

Reluctantly, Molly released his callused hand, feeling the roughness of his fingers against her palm as she turned loose.

"Be careful," she spoke quietly after him.

Reyes and Trace mounted their horses and turned away toward Moriarty.

Andy, disappointed that he was left at home, followed them to the hitching rail and stood holding Comet's reins. He supposed he would have to take the horse to water and put him out to pasture. He wanted, instead, to hop on his back and chase after Trace, but he knew he would only be turned back if he did. He watched the two men's backs diminish down the drive toward the main road.

Molly watched apprehensively from the window. She knew, one of these days, she would no longer be able to stop Andy. He would be right in the midst of things, with Trace, and she was afraid he was going to get hurt.

Letting go was painful and that time was coming soon.

Nineteen

When the posse reached Moriarty with Rigor and his gang in tow, the jail wagon still sat in front of the sheriff's office while Joe waited inside with a deputy.

Such a clatter of hoof beats came down the street that business owners and spectators came running to see what the excitement was about. The posse pulled up to the front of the office stirring up a dust cloud that swirled around the nearby onlookers.

Women fanned the dirt away from their faces with their hands and men wiped their sleeves across their foreheads to clear the dust from the sweat on their brows.

The sheriff and his deputies dismounted. Maria tossed her leg over Tom's horse's back so she could slide off on one side. Tom held her arm tight until she found her footing on the ground.

"Ma! Ma! Come quick," Elias called as he ran ahead of Shelia on the boardwalk.

"It's the man we had breakfast with. Mr. Tom. He's back and he's with a bunch of other men."

"Stay back, Elias." Shelia clutched the child's arm and pulled him to a safe distance.

Tom dismounted and moved to help the deputies take Rigor and his men into the jail.

Maria turned and saw Reyes and Trace riding toward them.

"Reyes! Reyes!" She shouted over the noise of the crowd. She stood on her tiptoes trying to flag him down over the crowd. Then, she stepped up onto a higher section of the boardwalk where she hoped her waving arms would be seen over the crowd that had gathered.

"Maria!" Reyes swung his horse's head to the side and rode up onto the boardwalk, crowding people aside. He reached down and lifted Maria up into his arms and sat her across his lap atop his horse.

"Where have you been, little sister?"

"Where have you been? Why did you not come and get me? What kind of a brother lets his little sister stay away from home so long?"

"I was trying to find you, little one. It has not been easy."

Maria put her arms around Reyes' neck. She wanted to cry but fought back the tears. He was here now and she was safe. That was all that mattered. She would have to tell him how near death she had come, but that would be some other time.

"*Madre* and *Padre*?"

"Aside from worry about you, they are fine."

Maria caught a glimpse of Tom looking her way. He stood outside the sheriff's office, letting the deputies secure the prisoners inside. The crowd was dispersing, from in front of the buildings, now. Trace had not dismounted and moved Lucky closer to Reyes and Maria.

"You had us worried, too, Maria," Trace said.

"I could not help it. Jesus came into the house and dragged me away. He said if I screamed, he would hurt your family. I had to go with him quietly."

Traced nodded.

"I understand. Well, thank goodness, everything has worked out all right. You will be going home to Mexico, now?"

"*Sí*," Maria felt a little sad. "I have grown to care about your family, as well, *señor* Trace. But Mexico is my home. Now that Reyes is here, I will go back."

"Of course you will," Reyes told her. "There is no question of that."

Tom approached the three of them cautiously.

"Trace," he greeted and reached a hand out.

"Well, Tom, you son-of-a-gun, it's good to see you." Trace dismounted and shook his hand again.

Tom looked at Reyes warily.

"You remember Reyes Espiañata, don't you, Tom?"

"Never met the man, but I recall chasing him and his *vaqueros* all the way to the *Rio Grande*. What are the two of you doing riding together after all the differences you've had?"

"Seems we had an interest in common. Maria showed up at our place, near dead, one day. Come to find out, she's Reyes' sister. He came looking for her. Once we straightened things out, we went to look for her together."

"I'm staying on the right side of the law in your country, now. All I want is to get my sister home. I'll settle things with Jesus some other time."

Tom let his comment settle in. He didn't fully trust the

man, but he would let things be and watch him for awhile.

"I'm headed back to Waco with this wagon here," Tom motioned toward the clumsy piece of machinery. "I'm taking the Bennington gang in. I'd appreciate it if you could ride along, Trace."

"Well, I'm a married man, now, Tom."

"I heard that."

"I don't think Molly'd like me taking off, clear over there right now."

"I'd see you got paid for your trouble."

"Thanks, Tom. I appreciate it. But, well, once you settle down, it takes a lot to pull you away from home."

"I heard tell that was the case, too."

"We'll be heading back to Mexico," Reyes broke into their conversation. "Normally, I do things on my own and in my own way. But, you people have saved my little sister. I'd ride along and keep an eye out for *banditos* to repay a debt owed you and *señor* Trace," Reyes offered.

Tom studied the man.

Maria spoke up for her brother, "You can trust Reyes to do as he says, *señor* Tom. You and *señor* Trace have saved me more than once. He will honor his debt to you."

Perhaps it would be better to have him on our side, rather than against us, Tom thought. *At least, with him riding along, I can keep an eye on him.*

"We will ride until the turn to Mexico," Reyes added.

"Agreed," Tom said.

"For this, you do not even have to pay me," Reyes stated.

Knowing that Reyes had profited in this country on other occasions, Tom accepted his offer.

"Mr. Tom! Mr. Tom," Elias shouted excitedly now that the crowd was gone and Sheila released him. He ran toward Tom.

Tom reached down and swung him into the air.

"Elias! How are you doing?" He set the child on his feet in front of him.

"I saw all the men come in. Did you capture all of them yourself?"

"No. I'm afraid not. I had some help." He looked at Maria. She watched the child with curiosity.

"Elias, come, we have business," Shelia spoke softly to her son.

"Afternoon, Shelia," Tom said. "This is my friend, Trace Westerman. And the gentleman on the horse is Reyes and the girl is his sister, Maria."

"Elias has an appointment to get some new clothes," Shelia explained. "There's a visiting tailor in town and Elias has outgrown all his pants." She didn't want to seem rude, so she explained their rush.

Elias looked up at Tom. He wrinkled his nose and pursed his lips. Getting measured for new clothes was the last thing he wanted to do today, but his mother would not let him get out of it.

Tom ruffled his hair with his heavy hand.

"We all need a new outfit, now and then," he told Elias.

Elias ran his index finger across the pearl handle on Tom's gun.

"It is nice to meet you all," Shelia said, "Now, please excuse us as I get Elias on to the tailor."

"Of course," Tom said.

"*Adios*, Elias, Shelia," Maria said.

"*Señora*," Reyes said.

"Ma'am," Trace added.

"Nice lady, Tom," Trace said.

Tom let his eyes follow Shelia and Elias' progress as they walked away toward the tailor's hotel room.

"Yeah. Seems real nice. Well, I better get on with what I've got ahead of me. Where can I find you when we're ready to leave, Reyes?"

"I will get Maria to the hotel. It looks like she could use some new clothes herself. While she buys a new dress, perhaps I can check the saloons and see if Jesus is keeping company with a *tequila* bottle."

"I'll look for you when we're ready to leave."

Trace reached out again to shake Tom's hand to say goodbye.

"I gotta get back to the farm, Tom. Stop by sometime, if you get back this way.

"Be sure to say 'hello' to Molly and the kids for me."

"Sure will." Trace got on Lucky and turned to leave. He couldn't help wanting to rush the horse down the street. He was careful not to crowd other riders. There would be time to run Lucky once he was off the main street and on the road home.

Twenty

Once Trace brought Andy home, Molly occupied the boy with all the chores that had been left undone while the two had been away. She planned to keep him busy enough he'd be distracted from following Trace and Reyes. She sent Seth to help Andy, knowing that he would run to tattle if Andy disappeared.

Rosie, relieved of her duties, went to her room where she felt she could safely unwind the stress that came from guarding her mind and tracking it on its human rail for so long. It seemed the episodes of slipping into a more natural-feeling feline state wanted to come more often now. She wondered how long she could continue to hide the condition from the family.

In the privacy of her own bedroom, she crawled beneath her bed bringing Callie along where they could snuggle in an old blanket she had snatched from Molly's trunk.

Soon, the two of them were fast asleep and, should Molly find her, she would be none the wiser. Rosie slipped from the feline posture into deep sleep where her brain relaxed and she would awake as that of a normal eleven-year-old girl. Although her more and more frequent diversions into a cat-like stance worried her, she carefully guarded her secret fearing no one would understand.

~ * ~

It was late the same evening of the day that Trace, Andy and Reyes had reached the house when Trace returned home alone.

All of the children, except Andy, were in bed. Molly and Andy waited for him, in the dim light of the kerosene lamp on the kitchen table, as Molly prepared a lesson plan for the following school year when she, once again, would be allowed to teach. Her opportunities were infrequent when she could work on the schedule for the new term and she stayed up beyond a normal bedtime, both to work and in anticipation of Trace's return.

Although Andy was old enough he could be allowed to drop out of his classes, Molly was determined that he would continue his schooling and she planned courses that were prerequisites to college in order to keep him challenged. She knew he would not be able to go away to school and had shown no desire to do anything except continue on with a farm life. His education would not be shallow through any fault of hers.

Already, other students his age in her school had turned to working at home or for a local business rather than pursue a higher education. Andy would not do that, if she could help it. She planned to teach him as long as she could.

Andy heard the sound of Lucky's hooves long before Trace reached the house. He jumped up and rushed to the door with Molly close behind him.

When Trace dismounted, Andy went to take the reins.

"I'll go unsaddle him and put him up for the night," Andy offered.

"Thanks. I appreciate that. It's been a long haul. I'm plain tuckered out."

"Is everything all right?" Molly asked as Trace dusted his hat across his pants leg before he entered the house. Crazy Leg nipped at the hat and tried to sink his teeth into its brim.

"Stop that, Crazy Leg!" Molly demanded.

Trace pushed the dog away and held his hat high while he went through the door and into the house.

"Get in here and settle down, if you're going to be inside tonight," he told the dog. "If you're going to act up, stay out. It's your choice."

The dog hung his head, like a naughty child, and walked slowly toward the rug in front of the fireplace. He hesitated a moment, then went to the stairs to go up and join Seth in his bed.

Trace shook his head.

"Sometimes that dog acts like he still thinks he's a pup."

Molly moved to get Trace a glass of milk. He looked hungry to her, so she dished stew up from the kettle at the back of the stove.

Trace sat down at the table across from her.

"Maria's with Reyes. They're heading back home to Mexico."

"I am so glad. How did you find her?"

"We didn't. Remember Tom, the Texas Ranger you

helped?"

"Of course."

"Well, he was back and got tangled up with a bunch that tried to help a prisoner, he was transporting, escape. Somehow, Maria managed to run into them and in the end, he brought her back to Moriarty. When we got there, there she was. She sent her thanks to you for helping her, too."

"The sheriff said Tom Jennings had passed through town. What happened to Maria? Where has she been?"

"Seems that *vaquero* that stole Comet some time back, decided to do the same with her. He slipped in here and took off with her. Reyes was right. It was Jesus."

"I'm glad she got away."

"Tom said to give you his greetings. He doesn't have time to stop. He promised a visit next time he comes through, though."

"If there is a next time," Molly said. "I'm surprised he was back here, now."

"I think he'll be back. I noticed he had a particular interest in a woman and her little boy in Moriarty. He didn't say anything, but he sure paid attention to what they were up to."

Molly smelled romance in the air and moved closer to Trace.

"I hope you encouraged him."

Trace laughed.

"I told him we were married. He didn't seem surprised. Think the sheriff had already filled him in."

The sound of Crazy Leg dropping to the floor overhead and his nails clipping across the wood, as he made his way around the bed to crawl back in on the other side, came to them.

"Seth must have kicked him to the floor," Trace commented.

"Sometimes Seth tosses and turns until the covers are on the floor and both of them might as well follow," Molly agreed.

Trace moved his chair back from the table and Molly situated herself on his lap while they talked.

It felt good to have someone to be close to, she thought and, although they tried not to become too affectionate in front of the children, they both enjoyed the loving touch of each other when they were alone.

Molly rubbed Trace's muscles between his shoulder blades.

"Trace, I'm really worried about Rosie." Little clues about the girl had been weighing heavily on Molly's mind and she needed to share her burden. She had had plenty of time to think about the problem on her ride into Moriarty in the buckboard. Now, she sought Trace's take on what her instinct told her might be a problem that she couldn't quite pin down.

"Why? She hasn't been having any of those spells where she predicts the future, again, has she?"

"No. But, she sometimes acts really strange. She thinks I don't notice, but I do. I just don't say anything."

"Strange? How?"

"I can't quiet put my finger on what's going on. She seems to lapse into a weird state and I have to, sometimes, call her name several times before she snaps out of it. What could it be, do you have any idea?"

"No. Maybe you should have Doc Landry take a look at her."

"I'm afraid this may not be something he can cure."

"Still, he'd know better than us, what's going on with her."

"Yes. I'll take her to see him as soon as I can." She leaned her face against the side of his head and felt the roughness of his unshaven cheek against her skin.

They sat that way a few seconds.

"I know you must be needing to get to bed," Molly finally broke the silence.

"It's been a really hard few days," Trace agreed. "And you need your rest. You might think you're as strong as you were before you got sick, but I'm not taking any chances."

Molly stood to let Trace get up.

Trace gently swatted her back side as she turned away.

~ * ~

When Molly took Rosie to see Doc Landry the girl was on her best behavior. She suspected something was on Molly's mind when she suggested the two of them ride into town while Trace and Andy stayed behind with the other children.

"Why are we going to town during the week, Ma?" Rosie wanted to know. The normal pattern for the family was to go together on a Saturday, especially when school was in session. That way, there was no rush to finish their errands before sunset.

"Since it's summer, we have all day to take care of things," Molly tried to explain. "I want you to see Doc Landry."

"But, I'm fine."

"You seem fine, Rosie. But, it's been a while since your accident. I think he should check you out."

Rosie cautioned herself. She would have to make sure she remained in what most people would consider a "normal" state. No cat activities today.

~ * ~

Doc Landry was finishing up setting a broken arm on one of the Johnson twins when Molly and Rosie walked into his office.

"Hello, Molly—Rosie," he greeted them. "What brings you two in?"

"I wanted you to take a look at Rosie."

Rosie hung back. She knew the Johnson boy and considered him mean. She didn't want to get near him, broken arm or not.

"Let me finish up here and we'll talk."

The Johnson boy dropped down off his seat on Doc's table.

"Run along and catch up with your Ma down at the General Store, now. Tell Mr. Newman I said to give you some candy on my account. He'll know what kind and how much."

"Yes, sir," the boy said, then turned and stuck his tongue out at Rosie.

He moved through the door letting it slam behind him.

Rosie made a face in the direction he had gone.

"Now, what did you have on your mind?" Doc Landry washed his hands and stood, wiping them on a towel.

"I wondered if you'd look at Rosie."

"What's wrong with her?"

"Rosie, go on outside for a bit. I'll call you back in when Doc's ready to see you."

"Yes, Ma." Rosie opened the door carefully, checking to see that the Johnson boy had gone on down the boardwalk toward the General Store before she went outside to sit on the wooden bench alongside the building.

Once she was out of earshot, Molly explained.

"I don't know what's wrong with her. Every once in a while she does the strangest things. Things she doesn't know I see."

"Like what? Does she get dizzy? Have headaches?"

"No. No symptoms that I can tell."

"She sometimes acts like—like she thinks she's a cat."

Doc studied Molly momentarily.

"I know it sounds strange, Doc. But, maybe she's copying Callie, I don't know. She curls up in the heat of the stove. She makes hissing noises and swipes her hands as if they were paws with claws on them."

Doc studied Molly with a puzzled expression on his face.

"I swear, sometimes she purrs."

"Have you ever talked to her about it?"

"No, of course not."

"Do you notice anything different about her right before she starts these actions?"

"No. Well, now that you mention it, she sometimes seems a bit dazed. Could it be from the wagon wreck, Doc?"

"I don't know. I've been reading up on studies about the mind. Reading about what makes people do things the way they do. I hate to tell you, Molly, but what I'm hearing doesn't sound good."

"What do we do, Doc?"

"Let me talk to her and see if I can get an idea about what's going on. Probably be best if I did it without you here. Do you have an errand you can run?"

"Oh, yes, if you think I should. She probably would feel more comfortable if I didn't stand here and listen."

Molly opened the door and called to Rosie.

"Doc's going to talk to you a little bit. While he does that, I'm going to pick up the grease Trace asked me to get for the wagon hubs. You wait here for me. I'll be right back."

"Yes, Ma."

Doc looked at this obedient little girl. She seemed so normal and compliant to him.

"Go ahead and climb up on the table, Rosie. I washed all those boy germs off there."

"Yes, sir."

Doc shoved a small wooden stool over in front of the table to assist her.

She stepped on it, then lifted her knee onto the table and turned to sit.

"Now, tell me, Rosie, how have you been feeling?"

"Fine."

"Nothing out of the ordinary? No more visions?"

"No." Rosie thought about the premonitions she had experienced in the past. She wished she did still get little glimpses of the future or thoughts when a loved one was in danger.

"Hmm." He looked in her eyes and pulled down the lower lids with his fingers. He felt for lumps on her skull and probed her mind with questions.

"Do you ever have strange feelings inside? Like your thoughts are somewhere outside your body?" Asking an eleven-year-old questions that could clue him into what was going on in her brain was difficult and he wondered how to pinpoint the problem.

"Sometimes, I feel like I am somewhere else looking down at myself."

"Like you are watching yourself move about?"

"Yes. Like I see my body move but I can't get my thoughts inside it."

Doc nodded.

"Do you ever see yourself as something else?"

"Sometimes I feel like I must be some other kind of thing. You know, like I'm a cat and I want to do cat things."

Doc quizzed her further.

"Like purring?"

"Yes. Or, curling up in a nice warm spot."

"And, do you carry out those actions?"

"Sometimes, I think so. I only know I feel that way and then something happens, and the feeling is gone, and Ma's standing over me asking me a question or telling me to do something."

"Does this happen very often?"

"Maybe once or twice a week."

"When was the last time you felt that way?"

"The other day when Ma came to town to look for Maria."

"And do you know if you followed through on your thoughts?"

"I knew I had to fight the voice inside me that was telling me I wanted to do that, because I was watching the babies."

"So, you can control this?"

"Sometimes. Sometimes I do things without even knowing I've done them."

Molly entered the office and Doc looked up.

"We're about through here. You can hop down, Rosie. Now, it's your turn. Run on over to the General Store and tell Mr. Newman to give you some candy on my account, too. You earned it."

"Thank you."

"You come right back here as soon as you get it, Rosie," Molly said.

Doc Landry waited until Rosie was well out of earshot. He stood back, leaned a hip against the examining table, and crossed his arms. He puzzled gravely over Rosie's disclosures.

"As you know, Molly, one of my big interests, since Rosie got injured, is the brain and how it works. We don't know a lot about it, yet. But, there are doctors that study people and there is a facility at Las Vegas for people whose minds have gone out of control."

"You're not saying Rosie's lost her mind, are you Doc?"

"I don't know what's going on. She seems to slip into a mental state where she feels that her mind and body separate. She admitted to lapses of time when she can't remember doing some of the things she does."

Molly studied the well-scrubbed floor.

"She says she has urges like a cat and that she doesn't

know whether she follows through with them or not."

"I know she sometimes does, Doc. I've seen her mimic Callie's actions. Maybe I should never have let her get the cat."

"I don't think that has anything to do with it. These books I've been reading—they say that sometimes people have what is called a "psychosis" where they think—they actually believe—they are an animal of some sort."

"Like a cat?"

"Or a chicken. Sometimes, they might even think they are a chicken and they will build a nest and walk in a squatted position clucking as if they were a hen."

"At least Rosie hasn't done that."

"Has she done anything to harm herself or anyone else?"

"No, not that I am aware of."

"Then, I'd talk to Trace. See what he thinks. If she's in no danger, then I'd say you can keep her home. But, I warn you, if she becomes a threat to herself or anyone else, even as young as she is, you may have to send her away."

"No! I can't send her away. How awful."

"Calm down, Molly. We'll just have to see what happens."

Rosie came back into the office. She carried a small brown bag with the allotted amount of candy inside. She looked at Molly and Doc Landry with curiosity.

"Well, we can head for home now, Rosie," Molly told her. "Doc says you're physically fit. Isn't that good news?"

Rosie nodded.

"I told you not to worry. I feel fine."

Molly cast a sideways glance at Doc and ushered the girl back outside to the buckboard.

The two of them climbed aboard and headed out of town. Molly was deep in thought, wondering what all this meant. Rosie was content to be sucking on the sweet treat Doc had so generously provided.

Neither of them mentioned what might lie ahead.

Twenty-one

The jail wagon lumbered along the hot, dry terrain of New Mexico. The pace was slow and, although Reyes and Maria could have ridden on ahead to speed up their trip to Mexico, Reyes kept his word and sat atop his horse alert to any signs of danger.

Reyes rode guard in front of the team that pulled the cumbersome wagon, which now held, not only Rigor, but three members of his gang. He scouted ahead looking for trouble, and reported back to Tom what he saw. So far, his reports had been mundane and the trip was going well.

Inside the steel-skinned coach, Rigor kept his silence trying to sleep but awakening with each jolt of the uncomfortable stage. Busy dreaming up a way to escape, when he didn't doze, he remained oblivious to the discomforts and comments of his men.

Maria had abandoned her horse for a more comfortable ride atop the coach with Joe.

Tom rode behind at a short distance, leading Maria's steed, and keeping a careful watch on the travelers ahead of him. Eating dust was not his preference but he felt it would be to his advantage, if someone tried to stop the coach, to have a full view of what went on. Rigor was not going to escape this time, if he could help it. It was a long way to Waco and he felt his vigilance was necessary.

Tom paced his horse behind the jail wagon, keeping enough distance between them to be sure he could always have it in sight. Occasionally, his mind drifted back to thoughts of the woman he had met in Moriarty, Shelia, and her son, Elias. He felt a gnawing in his gut to want to settle down. To have a family, if not children of his own, then a child that needed the strong hand of a man—a child that might grow up too soft under the supervision of a woman alone. The West was dangerous. By the time he had reached the age of fifteen, he was already on his own and having to defend himself with a pistol. When he was eighteen, he had felt it was best to stay on the right side of the law and joined the Texas Rangers. He'd been a Ranger ever since that time.

It was a dilemma, to him, how he liked the softness of the woman, yet knew, instinctively, the boy would have to toughen up. He only hoped it was not too late. Even as he rode the distance between Moriarty and Waco, he was formulating a plan.

He had some money saved up. He'd planned to buy a ranch when he stopped riding for the Rangers. He'd planned to settle down and raise horses and cattle. If he handled it just right, he might be able to make that happen sooner, rather than later. He might be able to return to New Mexico and buy a small piece of land—build a cabin and stock the land with enough animals to support himself and a budding family. He felt an unusual stirring inside his gut. He wanted to settle down. Now. If Shelia would agree to it, he'd ask her to marry him.

Tom was feeling too cozy with his new plans. He was seeing a different world in his mind than the one they were currently traveling through when a gun's blast shattered his thoughts.

Joe fired an answering volley with the shotgun.

Tom jerked to attention on the first sound and spurred his horse forward before the second.

"What is it?" He called to Joe.

"Don' know."

The horses were jerking nervously in their traces as Tom raced past them.

Reyes, his pistol still in the air from the warning shot, ran his horse toward Tom and skidded to a stop.

"There's a band of renegades ahead," he turned his horse and shouted toward the oncoming wagon. "Maria, get down below the foot boards. Find a rifle. Be ready!"

Joe raised his shotgun in the air to show the other men he was prepared.

Reyes turned his horse to ride alongside Tom while they discussed their defense.

"What do you think? Shall we hole up here and wait for them to come to the wagon?" Tom asked.

"There's about eight of them in full war paint," Reyes filled him in.

"I thought things were peaceful out here, now."

"We can try to run through them, but I don't think we'd have a chance, *amigo*."

"We're only four guns to eight of them."

"I only saw a couple of rifles in the bunch. Mostly, knives and bows and arrows."

"They're just as deadly, if they're aim is good." Tom held his pistol in his left hand now, hefting it to fine-tune its balance in his hand.

"It's your call, *amigo*—your prisoners. Maria is a good shot. I taught her well."

"I figure, our best chance is to rush them. It'll be harder for them to aim with their bows if we're moving, than if we're sitting ducks. All they'd have to do is pick off the horses and we'd be stuck anyway."

What had been only a few moments before an almost pleasant ride, now caused Tom's insides to twist and turn like someone was tying sausage in its casing. He didn't like putting Maria at risk, or any of them for that matter, except Rigor and his cronies. Either way they turned, they were going to have to fight. For once, he was glad Reyes was on his side. He knew he would fight to his death to see that his sister survived.

Tom raised his right arm and signaled Joe to rush the horses, full speed, ahead.

Reyes fell in on one side of the team and Tom on the other. They both held the reins of their mounts in their fingers below their gun butts so they could fire when necessary.

As they entered the area Reyes had indicated the renegades were waiting, Tom saw nothing. He looked over at Reyes with a questioning look.

Reyes' glance back toward him showed just as much surprise.

Where did they go?

"There's a town up ahead about six more miles," Tom shouted. "If we can run the team that far, we'll be safe."

Reyes nodded.

Tom looked back at Joe to see that he kept the horses racing toward the town.

Tom saw Reyes take aim toward the wagon and fire.

"What the hell?" Tom wondered aloud, at first thinking Reyes was firing at Joe.

A brave, in full war paint, tumbled from the right rear corner of the wagon into the dust behind it.

Tom now realized the renegades had taken the time to circle back and come up from behind them. Two of them ran their ponies close enough to the wagon to grasp ahold of the top rail and spring onto the careening coach.

Shooting behind them without being able to take aim properly at the Indians, while running their horses, was difficult for the two men. Joe grappled with the reins and tried to balance the heavy shotgun on his arm, while controlling the team, in case he needed to fire it.

Tom saw two more painted bodies toss their legs over the rear corner of the wagon and start to make their way toward Joe and the space where Maria crouched below the wagon top. One carried a knife in his left hand while he held tight to the open window rim near the coach's roof. One of the prisoners inside pried at his fingers trying to loosen his grip. The second Indian moved along the right edge of the top toward Maria's hiding place. Tom could see the end of her rifle barrel sticking above the front edge of the wagon top and pointed toward the rear.

The ruckus the equipment made covered any noise that came from directly behind them. Joe was unaware of the impending danger to the rear. If the Indian reached him with the knife, Joe could die and the wagon would be out of control and headed for destruction.

Reyes slowed his horse to let the team catch up.

Tom did the same.

If he was going to end up in hand-to-hand combat, Tom would do what he could to shoot as many renegades as possible.

Tom heard one of the prisoners yelp and saw blood where the Indian had used his knife to release the prisoner's grip on his fingers. Free now to move forward, the Indian raised to a squatted position, beginning to upright himself. The wagon lurched, throwing him off balance and sending him sprawling across the top of the metal roof and off the back of the wagon.

Reyes was close enough now to take aim at the second Indian and his accurate shot dislodged him from the wagon top as well.

The distance between the other five Indians and the wagon was such that Reyes turned back to follow the coach up close. He fired behind him without being able to take careful aim. He could only hope his bullets would hit their mark, or that the renegades would drop back further to avoid being shot.

Tom, unable to shoot because of Reyes' position between the wagon and the Indians, kept watch and paced his horse alongside the wagon.

An arrow whizzed past his right knee and he sensed the aim could have been for either him or Reyes. They were in a bad position, so close together with him alongside the lumbering wagon and Reyes at the rear. Still, there was nowhere to go without leaving the wagon less protected.

"Toss us some weapons," Rigor shouted. "Don't leave

us in here to die helpless."

Tom ignored his call.

If Joe could put some more distance between the wagon and the Indian ponies, they might have a chance.

Tom fired into the air, over the team's head, hoping to startle the horses into a faster pace.

Joe whipped the reins across the horse's backs and called out, "Yeaaaaah!"

Now, Tom could see the town far off in the distance ahead. Surely, the renegades wouldn't risk getting too close to town where reinforcements could cut them off.

When Tom looked back again, Reyes was flat against his great black horse's neck. He created as small a target as he could and fired his gun behind him without looking.

Gradually, the Indian ponies slowed as the wagon raced on toward town.

Tom could see the remaining attackers gathered in a circle behind them now, their animals prancing about as they sucked air into their nostrils and their sides heaved.

When they had put enough distance between them and danger, Tom signaled Joe to rein in the team. As the team slowed its pace, Maria, rifle still in her hands, uncurled herself from below in the front of the wagon box and dragged herself back up to the seat.

Reyes pulled his horse out from behind the wagon and came up alongside Tom once more. He re-holstered his pistols.

"I have not had that close a call in a long time *mi amigo*."

"Nor, I." Tom remembered the time he and Reyes' had been on opposite sides of the law. One of Reyes' *vaqueros* had stolen Andy Kling's horse. He and Trace Westerman had chased them back to the Mexico border. He wondered if Reyes was recalling that time as well.

Joe halted the coach and sat waiting for Tom and Reyes to approach them.

Reyes rode up to the passenger side of the wagon while Tom came alongside the small window where blood now stained the metal.

"Are you all right, Maria?"

"*Sí*, Reyes. I am a bit shaken up by the rough ride and frightened by the close call."

"What about inside there," Tom asked his prisoners.

"We got the bleeding stopped. Don't think he'll lose any fingers," Rigor answered for his gang member.

"Fine. Then we'll stop at this town we're coming to and get some food and rest."

"Sounds good to me," Joe added. He rubbed his arm across his brow letting the dirt and sweat soak into the back of his shirtsleeve. "I could use a drink and I don't mean water from that canteen back there."

He called to the horses to start forward again, moving ahead at a slower pace.

When they reached the shingle, nailed to a post and set into the dirt at the side of the road, they read the town's name crudely printed on its face. Heaven's Gate. The word "Heaven's" had been crossed out with an "X". The word "Hell's" was scrawled at an angle above it. It was tightly squeezed to fit on the board

"Hell's Gate. Now, I wonder what that means," Tom said to no one in particular.

Reyes shrugged. He cared less, as long as they could

get what they needed, rest a bit and move on.

As they rode into town, the only noise they heard was that of their own team and wagon. The slight jingle of metal rings and spurs and creaking of leather saddles and traces were eerie sounds to their ears.

They saw no one.

The town appeared deserted.

Twenty-two

Joe halted the wagon at the beginning of the main street.

He stared in disbelief, as did Tom, Reyes and Maria. All four tried to figure out why they saw no horses—no humans—no activity of any kind. The silence was so acute they could hear themselves breathe. They looked at one another with questioning expressions.

What is wrong here?

"Hey!" Rigor called out through the small barred window, breaking the silence. "What's going on? Why are we stopped?"

Then he, too, was quiet.

One of his cohorts started to ask a question and he shushed him.

Down the street, where the buildings covered only a few short blocks, not a living thing stirred. Not a bird, a dog or a being of any kind.

A sudden gust of wind rattled a strip of tin across the boardwalk, out into the street and across to the other side where it stuck, on edge, between the slits of lumber that served as a walkway. It caught at the bottom and the long thin piece of tin shuddered in the breeze producing an eerie trembling tone like someone playing a bow across a handsaw.

A slight odor reached Tom's nose. It was putrid and he had smelled it before.

Maria pulled the scarf she had bought in Morarity from around her neck and wrapped the thin material across her nose and mouth.

Reyes glanced at Tom with a knowing look.

"Hey, get us out of here. The heat and that stink is going to make us puke," Rigor called out callously.

"I smell death. This town's been hit by sickness, or something," Joe said.

"I'm thinking the same thing," Tom agreed.

The last building on the main street, was a church. Its whitewashed steeple, as opposed to the weathering wood on the other buildings, stood out as a beacon to lead its followers in the right direction.

"You keep the rig here," Tom told Joe. "Maria, you stay here with Joe. Reyes and I'll each take one side of the street and check the buildings out. If it's safe, we'll let you know."

Tom and Reyes dismounted wrapping the reins of their horses at the nearest hitching rail.

Reyes went into the first building on the right with his guns drawn. He pushed the swinging door of the saloon open with the palm of one hand while he kept his pistols ready in the fingers of both.

Tom, his mother-of-pearl-handled revolver in his left hand turned the doorknob of the General Store. It was a narrow building on the left side of the street.

They were gone but a few minutes before they were both back out in the street consulting on what they had seen.

"It's like they picked up very little and left," Tom said.

"Only partially filled bottles of liquor sat on the shelf behind the bar," Reyes said.

"Then, the proprietor must have taken the full ones and left the others behind. They didn't want to waste any time."

Tom raised his eyebrows as if to ask the question that was on both their minds.

"No bodies," Tom said.

"Not in there, either," Reyes tossed his head toward the saloon. "There were chairs, tables and half-empty bottles. Cards were dumped on the floor and stuff looked like it had been blown around for awhile."

"No sign of Indians," Tom added. "So, they must not have been raided."

They went on to the next buildings only to find the same story at each abandoned establishment.

When they reached the church, they went in together.

Reyes knelt at the doorway and crossed himself as they entered, then clutched his hand across his nose and mouth.

Tom pulled his neckerchief up over the tip of his nose.

The two men's eyes met. This was the location from where the stench was emanating.

They walked down the short center isle toward the pulpit, dreading what they felt lay ahead.

As they reached the small table where a bible lay, they saw a writing quill and a bottle of ink. The ink bottle was on its side and the liquid had spilled out and dried in a splotch across the white linen tablecloth.

The cloth reached all the way down the table legs to the floor.

At the narrow end of the table, the soles of a pair of boots stuck out and Tom knew they had to be on somebody's feet—feet that were not going anywhere.

Tom stepped around the edge of the table.

There, lying on the floor dressed in a black suit was what had once been the town's preacher.

"How many days you figure?" Tom asked Reyes when he joined him.

"Hard to say, *amigo*," Reyes spoke softly. "It is bad luck to kill a man of God."

"It doesn't look like he died from a gunshot or arrow," Tom said, using the toe of his boot to nudge the body to look for wounds.

He looked about for any other clues that would indicate how the man died.

He set the ink jar upright, then realized the answer might lie in the pages of the Bible. He picked it up and leafed through the Book. In the back was a blank page with lines to record births and deaths. The latest entry on the births was that of an infant, yet unnamed, Pastor Smith and mother, White Dove Smith, dated less than a week ago.

Then an entry in a shaky hand stated, "All parishioners gone. I feel the effects of the illness that has plagued this town."

Tom heard a slight noise off to his right.

"What was that?"

"Sounded like a cat sneezing," Reyes dismissed it.

Tom read on.

"Wife gave birth. Too weak to help her."

A long heavy line ran down the page and off onto the white tablecloth.

"Some sort of sickness overtook 'em, I guess," Tom said. "I'll set the prisoners to burying him and then we'll get out of here before one of us comes down with it."

The noise persisted behind the door on the right.

Tom cocked his gun and moved toward the sound.

Reyes followed close behind him.

When Tom opened the door, cautiously, the noise became more audible.

"A *bebé*!" Reyes announced.

There a tiny infant lay cradled in its mother's arms where she lay across a small pallet on the floor. Against the wall was a newly beaded cradleboard, its leather fresh and unsoiled.

Tom moved forward and saw the woman stared straight at the ceiling with unseeing eyes. Tom closed the woman's eyelids.

"I'd say she hasn't been dead for long. What do you think? Is she Sioux or Cherokee?"

Reyes shrugged.

"This might explain why we ran into those Indians back there. They're as scared of disease as we are. They could have come after her and backed off when they sensed the town was sick."

Tom removed the baby from its mother's stiff arms and wrapped its blanket closer around the squirming arms and legs.

"What do we do with a *bebé*?" Reyes asked.

"I don't know, yet, but we can't leave it here to starve or get sick and die like its folks. There were a few cans of food in some of those stores, maybe we can find something that will work for milk somewhere." Tom worried. *How are we going to feed a tiny baby?* He knew very little about things like that.

"Grab that Bible over there, would you? If I study it later, it might tell us if this baby has any family."

They walked out of the church and headed down the street, back toward the wagon. Tom carried the bundle carefully in his right arm while he kept his left arm ready for action if any more surprises awaited them.

Maria burst into a run when she saw them coming. She looked surprised when she saw the squirming infant in Tom's arm.

"A *bebé*," she muttered almost in reverence.

Tom handed the child to her.

"You probably know more about caring for this than I do."

He purposely avoided telling her the circumstances of finding the child.

"We'll look for some Borden's and something we can fix into a bottle. I'm sure we can find some kind of clean cloth to wrap it in, even if it isn't a regular baby gown or blanket. I don't think we should leave it in its swaddling." Tom was as much concerned about germs, that might have spread from the sickness of the baby's mother, as he was the soiling from the baby itself.

Maria gently cuddled the baby and tried to quiet it.

"I'm sure it's hungry," Tom informed her. He turned to Joe. We'll be here a bit. Might as well unhitch the team and see if you can find anything for the horses to eat. I saw a watering trough alongside one of the buildings in the shade. Reyes," Tom tossed the key to the jail wagon to him, "you let the prisoners out and keep an eye on them. Head them on down to take care of that detail we were talking about as soon as they've stretched their legs."

"Maria, you come with me. Let's see if we can find something to make the little one more comfortable and fill its belly."

The words of fear remained unspoken. None of them wanted to hang around a town where the chance of catching the illness was still a possibility. Yet, uppermost in some of their minds, at this time, was seeing that the infant survived.

At the General Store, Maria found some soft, light-colored cloth to use as diapers. She handed the baby to Tom, then, unrolled the bolt of fabric and spread it out.

The bundle felt light in his arm and he sensed a warmth inside his chest he had never known before. He lifted his index finger, large alongside the infant's tiny fist, and the baby soon gripped his finger as if holding on to its only hope for life.

Tom whispered softly to the baby, half embarrassed that Maria might hear.

"Don't you worry, little one. We're going to see that you are safe."

Maria measured out lengths of the cloth from her hand to her elbow, then tore an edge with her front teeth and pulled the fabric apart to make squares.

She piled them on the table as she tore them until she had a stack she thought would do.

"There were some canned goods over there," Tom motioned with a nod of his head. He was reluctant to give the baby back to Maria and waited for her to search for a way to feed the little creature. "Look for a can with the drawing of a cow's head on the paper. If Borden's was good enough for the Civil War soldiers, it ought to work for her."

She found a can of peaches and set it aside.

"We can use those ourselves," she said, still studying the crude images on the rough paper labels attached to the cans.

"Might as well take what we need," Tom agreed.

The baby fussed and Tom jiggled it up and down hoping to quiet it until it could be fed.

Maria moved to another area of the store and studied the bottles sitting empty on the shelf. She selected two that were small and could be used to hold milk, if they found some. If they didn't, she didn't know what they would do. *How will we feed a bebé when there is nothing around that gives milk?*

"This is a store," she said, "there must be something here somewhere that will work."

"It looks like the owner only took what he thought was too important to leave behind."

Maria rummaged through a small wooden box. At last, she found one nipple that could be stretched over a bottle.

She held it up and looked at it.

"Well, this is what we want." But, when she went to put it on one of the bottles she already had, she found the opening on the glass was too wide to stretch the nipple over it. She abandoned the bottles and went back to the shelf.

"A whiskey bottle," Tom said.

"What??"

"I bet it would fit on a whiskey bottle."

"You're probably right. And, the alcohol would have killed the germs. I'll be right back." Maria ran to the saloon next door and soon returned with two half-empty bottles.

She stood outside and poured the liquor into the dust on the street.

Joe saw her dump the alcohol and cringed. *Women have no idea how important a drink can be to a man.* He hoped there would be some left when he got the horses watered. Surely, Maria wouldn't dump all the bottles.

She went back inside.

"I saw a well down by the church. Maybe there's a bucket there, too. I'll see if I can find something to carry water back in and get some for you to clean the baby up."

"I'll need to rinse the bottles, a bit, so the *bebé* doesn't get too much taste of the whiskey. Now, if I can find some canned milk—"

Maria took the baby from Tom and he surrendered it reluctantly.

"I'll look on my way to the well. There were a couple other stores that seemed like they had some general merchandise in them. Maybe I can find a bucket there. Perhaps some milk, too."

"I certainly hope so. This little one would be crying more if it had the energy, I think."

Poor thing! Tom hurried out the door, then turned when he saw the activity at the church. Rigor and his three men were bringing a body out wrapped in a blanket. Reyes stood right behind them, both pistols aimed in their direction.

"You stay here. I'll bring what I can find back to you," Tom said, hoping to keep Maria from seeing the scene in the churchyard.

The people had left in such a panic they had taken very little with them. Tom soon returned with a pail of water and a basket, loaded with supplies, on his other arm.

He smiled at Maria broadly.

"Milk," he announced as he displayed the can with a crude sketch of a cow's head and the words "Canned Milk" printed on its paper label. "Fresh water. And, I found that one of the stores had living quarters in the back. They must have had a young one, because I found these baby clothes left behind and a fresh blanket."

"Good," Maria said. "I put a clean cover on her bottom, but she could use a bath. Now, leave us while we do girl things and I figure out how to feed her."

"The writing on the label says the contents have to be diluted. Half and half, it says."

"Thank you, now, go."

Tom left to check on Joe and the progress of the burials.

Joe had found a shaded area between the buildings where the water trough was kept filled by a trickle of water from a rare underground spring situated next to a livery stable. There was grass there, in a small quantity, but it was enough to occupy the team for the moment.

He could hear the baby screaming in the store where he had left Maria to care for her.

The bath Maria is giving her probably isn't warm enough to her liking. And the milk, likewise, probably doesn't suit her, he suspected. He only hoped she would be too hungry to mind a lot.

He saw Reyes sitting on the church steps now as Rigor and his men took turns digging with the only shovel they could find. Reyes leaned his forearms across his knees with both pistols still in his hands.

"Do you want me to watch them for a bit?"

"Nah, *amigo*, I've gotten used to the smell now. How is the *bebé*?"

"Maria is doing a fine job with her. Once she gets some food in her belly, she should come around just fine."

"Maria has always been good with the *niño*s," *Reyes* agreed. "She will make a good mother some day. If I can keep the coyotes away from her until she finds a proper young man to marry."

He thought about Jesus and felt anger well inside him. *If it hadn't been for the renegade vaquero, I and Maria would be back in Mexico where we belong. My little sister would not be exposed to all the dangers we have run into.* It made him angrier to think about Jesus and he took his frustration out on the prisoners by yelling at them.

"You. Dig harder," he shouted to one of Rigor's men. "You want to be here all day? Maybe catch whatever it is that killed him?"

The man did not answer but gouged the shovel deeper into the gritty dirt.

Rigor glanced at Reyes with anticipation in his eyes. *The time was right. They were out in the open, now. No more chains or being locked up in the wagon. If I can escape, I'll not be going back into that bake oven.*

He watched for an opportunity to make a break.

~ * ~

The basket Tom had carried the supplies in was big enough for Maria to spread the clean blanket inside and put the freshly washed and fed baby in it. She found a flour sack and packed the extra clothes, diapers and bottle in that. Then she found a small wooden crate and put what canned goods she had gathered in it along with the canned milk Tom had found in another location.

The baby slept peacefully, now, and Maria called to Joe to help her with the supplies.

"Sure hope you didn't toss all that booze out, Miss," Joe said when he came through the door.

"I'm sure you'll find more where that came from." *Men and their thirst for the burning liquid that makes them crazy,* Maria thought but kept her silence. She knew Joe had a hard job and depriving him of a small pleasure was not something she wanted to do.

"Soon as I get this stuff to the wagon, I'm going to find out. I don't like the taste, nor smell, of this town."

Joe hefted the box of supplies in his hands and walked toward the door. Maria slid one arm through the handle of the baby's basket and grasped the top of the flour sack with the other. She couldn't wait to get out of this town, either.

Suddenly, shots rang out and Maria ducked behind the wagon with the baby, dropping the sack of clothes in the dirt.

"What's going on?" Joe called out.

Reyes' guns repeated their first burst.

Tom, squatting behind a rain barrel next to the church, called back, "Rigor just made a break for it."

Joe dropped low and headed for Tom with the shotgun in his hand.

When the shooting stopped, Tom crept around the barrel.

"You stay here and keep these other three under guard, Joe. Matter-of-fact, take them on back to the wagon until I can lock 'em up. Reyes still has the key so you'll have to stick something through the latch to hold 'em. I don't figure they'll argue with your scatter gun much. I'll go after Rigor."

He piled over the top of the grave where the men had heaped dirt after dumping both bodies into one hole. Keeping shelter between him and the direction in which Rigor had run off, he edged his way around a building and peered into a fenced backyard.

Rigor was nowhere in sight.

He's got to be lying low in a ditch or something, Tom thought. *There's no where for him to hide out here.*

The surrounding terrain was flat without a tree in sight. If the Indians were still out there, there would be no chance for a man alone to survive against them.

I should let him go and meet his fate, Tom thought. *It would save the state of Texas the money to feed him for the rest of his life, if he doesn't hang.* But, then, it would also mean he failed his mission and he couldn't bear to think of that.

Already, the idea of resigning from the Texas Rangers was forming in Tom's head along with thoughts of settling down. He was sick of chasing after outlaws and hauling them in for prosecution. Half the time, they'd get off and he'd be out chasing them again the next time they broke the law. *What's the point?*

He thought of Shelia and Elias, then he shook his head to clear it. *I have to focus on Rigor and recapturing him. I can't risk being caught off guard.*

He saw a movement off to his left and sucked his body back against the building, waiting to see what it had been.

He held his pistol close to his chest and kept the barrel out of the sun to avoid a glint that would expose him.

"*Amigo*," Reyes called out. "You need help?"

Tom didn't answer. To do so would only show Rigor his position.

He could hear the horses being moved into their traces in front of the wagon as Joe readied the team for the next leg of their journey.

Reyes, noting a slight shadow alongside the building, found another secure site and waited.

Rigor, unaware of Tom's location, broke into a run. He headed back toward the trail, out of town, in the direction they had come.

Tom fired his pistol.

He heard a groan.

He had aimed low, hoping to stop Rigor, not kill him. He didn't relish a ride on into Waco with a dead body. He'd had enough stench in his nostrils for awhile.

Rigor grasped his leg and tried to continue limping away from town.

"One more step and I'll shoot to kill," Tom warned him.

"If he doesn't, I will," Reyes added as he cocked both

guns and took aim.

Tom approached Rigor cautiously.

The bullet had found a fleshy area near his leg's calf muscle and, although painful, the wound would not be fatal.

"You'll live to see Waco," Tom said when he inspected the wound.

Rigor scowled in his direction.

"I just saved you from a more painful death," Tom said. "Those Indians out there don't want the sickness from this town brought out to them. They'd see you didn't get far. Now, get up and head back to the wagon with the others."

Reyes tossed Tom the key ring.

He caught it with his right hand and prodded Rigor with the pistol in his left.

"It's time we got out of here," Tom said.

Twenty-three

As the small group of people left the town behind, they heard shouts of Indians as they rode their ponies quickly past the wooden buildings. They shot their arrows with burning moss tied to them into the structures as they raced by.

Tom was sure they were under orders of their Medicine Man to dispose of the white man's disease.

As they watched, they saw the town become a roaring inferno. Heaven's Gate was sure to be erased from the landscape of the prairie.

Later that night when they had traveled far enough away from the town, and the threat of Indian attack, they made a campfire and prepared to rest and eat.

Maria, having set the baby in its basket by her feet in the passenger side at the top of the wagon while they rode, found the ride rather likable to the infant. She had slept most of the way, waking only to take more nourishment midway through their journey.

Now, a campfire blazed and all had warm food in their bellies.

Rigor and his men were still locked inside the wagon

as Tom had no intention of tracking any of them down again.

He came toward the fire, now, approaching where Maria sat with the baby, in its bed, alongside her.

"What do you have there?" Maria asked as Tom reached her side.

"Apparently the preacher was writing something in this Bible when he dropped. Figure it might give us an idea what to do with the baby."

Maria nodded. She was accustomed to people keeping family records in Bibles. It was a practice started by the *Padres* as documentation that would not be disputed.

Tom squatted before the fire, letting the bright flames illuminate the carefully written words in the front of the Book.

"Jeremiah Smith married White Dove, daughter of a Cherokee Chief. Most of her people were wiped out by sickness. Figure fear of disease by the remaining members of the tribe is probably the only reason they haven't come to take her back."

"That explains why we ran into those Indians back there," Tom said. "Chances are she still has some family that didn't like the idea of her marrying a white man and they were coming to get her."

Beyond that, Smith had written his parent's names, dates of birth and dates of their deaths in less legible script. He listed no brothers or sisters. No other relatives.

"Well," Tom said, "it appears the baby has no one to take her. Surely, the tribe wouldn't want her because of her mother's history. Still, she was a chief's daughter— I'd almost bet the bunch we ran into were part of her tribe."

"No relatives to take care of her," Maria repeated sadly. "Well, if there is no one to name her, than we must. We can't keep calling her "*bebé*." Maria told the group. "She must have a name. She must have a christening."

"We're only one day, or so, away from Waco," Tom said. "We need to make a more important decision. What are we going to do with her?"

"*Sí*," Reyes agreed with his sister. "A christening is necessary. In Mexico, sometimes families are *mucho*, one more *niño* seems like nothing. Perhaps, we could find someone there to take her," Reyes offered.

Maria cuddled the infant.

"She could be a little sister, Reyes." Already she was growing attached to the child. For the first time in her life, someone needed her. *It is a good feeling.*

"Ah, any mission that has Sisters, usually has an orphanage, too," Joe suggested. "You could always take her to one of them."

"I don't think so. She needs a real family," Tom said, feeling paternal toward the infant. He didn't mention that he already had a plan forming in his own mind.

"Let us take her to Mexico," Maria pleaded.

"Seems to me," Joe piped up, "that she belongs in this country." He peeked at her small face as she slept peacefully. "She's one tough 'lil *hombre*."

"You ever get married and have any kids, Joe?" Tom asked as he leaned back on his elbow and enjoyed the heat of the fire.

"Nah, no woman ever'd want to put up with an old

mule skinner like me." He touched the baby's fist with his coarse finger.

Tom saw there was a softness beneath Joe's rough exterior.

"Near had me one, onct, though. Sweetest little thing you ever did see. I's a little shaver, myself, back then. Growin' nothin' but peach fuzz on my face, but she sure did turn my head." Joe stroked his full beard as he recalled his past. He looked off into the flames of the fire as if seeing her face, again.

"Yeah. I'm thinking maybe we tend to wait too long, sometimes. I've never been married, either. But, you know what? I'm fixing to change all that," Tom said and looked at Maria.

"Remember that woman, and her son, I introduced you to back in Moriarty? Well, I think her boy could use someone to teach him how to be a man. Think, since she's already got one kid, maybe she wouldn't mind having another one. What woman could turn down a sweet little bundle like that, anyway?"

Disappointment creased Maria's face.

"You're not much more than a *niño*, yourself," Reyes reminded his sister. "Someday, you'll get married and have *bebés* of your own. It is probably best the *bebé* stays here, on this side of the *Rio Grande*."

"When we get to Waco and get these prisoners locked up, I'll turn in my badge. You've been a big help, Reyes. No hard feelings about the past. You've saved our bacon a time or two this trip. You and Maria will probably be anxious to get on over the border and back home to your parent's ranch."

"When you check in, I'll be getting another Ranger escort, in Waco, to go on to Missouri and pick up more prisoners," Joe said.

Reyes unfolded the length of his legs in the heat from the fire. He stretched his saddle blanket out and situated the saddle's seat beneath his head. He laid back and tipped his *sombrero* over his face.

Maria put the baby back in its basket and found a comfortable position for herself. There was no use arguing with these three men over where the *bebé* would end up. Reyes was probably right, she would, someday, bear her own *bebés*. Joe seemed to sense that the child might be looked upon as different among countrymen that were not her own. It was probably best that she go with Tom. She felt a tug at her heart. Funny how something so tiny could have such an effect on women. And, on men, too. Here she was thinking of having *bebés* of her own and everyone else, except Reyes, was mooning around like they were experiencing a miracle.

She wondered about her brother. Why was he speaking less of the child's future than the other men? Perhaps because he was already engaged and expected to start a family of his own soon? Knowing her brother, and his larcenous ways in the past, she wondered. *Does he plan to steal the bebé and take it to Mexico, anyway? Would he do as Jesus had, when he stole Andy's horse because he thought he could buy her affection? In the past, Reyes saw to it that she had whatever she wanted.*

She knew, if he tried to take the baby with them, there would be a blood bath. She could tell Tom would not give the child up easily. She would have to convince

Reyes she did not want the *bebé* bad enough for him to do anything dangerous.

She lay on the hard ground, trying to fall asleep and wondering how she could do that.

Twenty-four

The next morning they broke camp after breakfast. Tom pushed some hard tack through the bars of the jail wagon and gave the prisoners water from canteens. One by one, Reyes guarded each of them as they were allowed to move into the bushes and relieve themselves before the last leg of the journey.

Few words were spoken amidst the three men, Tom, Reyes and Joe.

Maria sensed a tension in the air.

When Reyes locked the padlock on the wagon and handed the key back to Tom, Maria jerked her head to signal him she wanted to talk.

He ignored her.

When she had a chance to get closer to him, she whispered, "Talk to me, Reyes. What are you planning to do?"

"What do you mean, *niño*?"

"Don't call me '*niño*'. I am a young woman, now. You must treat me with more respect. Besides, that's not what I want to talk about."

"So, what do you want to talk about?"

"I saw that look on your face last night right before you covered it with your *sombrero*."

Reyes showed no expression on his face now. It was something he had practiced doing to fool his opponents.

"Reyes! Listen to me! If you think I can not live without taking this *bebé* back to Mexico, you are wrong."

Reyes looked surprised.

"I might have been a spoiled *niño* that got everything I wanted in the past. But, I have learned life doesn't accommodate all your wishes. I told you, I am a young woman now. I know we have to do what is best for the child. Not what I want."

Reyes looked at his sister with more respect than he had ever felt for her.

"Once we ride out of Waco, whatever we do, there will be no turning back," he told her.

"I would rather ride out of town, just the two of us, than to have you dead in the street for trying to take this *gringo's* child. Don't you see he's made up his mind? If we try to ride off with her, he will kill you, or die trying."

"Ah, Maria, you are growing up. No longer can Reyes buy your affection with gifts."

"You don't need to, my brother. We will always be family. This *bebé* needs its own family."

"Perhaps you are right."

Reyes walked away and tightened the cinch on his horse. He slowly climbed up into the saddle.

Maria handed the handle of the basket to Joe. When he had the wicker basket settled securely on the footboards, he reached a hand down to help Maria up to sit beside him.

"I'm going to scout up ahead," Tom said. An uneasy feeling had been haunting him ever since they had left Heaven's Gate—or Hell's Gate—depending on who you believed, behind them. A time or two he could have sworn he saw the flick of a figure crouched behind a sagebrush. Once the birds had scattered, off to their left side, when they were far enough away they should not have taken notice of them.

Tom moved ahead of the wagon cautiously, checking every mound of dirt and clump of sage that he passed.

Something wasn't right. He sensed it.

As he walked his horse ahead, he turned to see that the wagon was still in sight and in no danger before he edged further down the trail.

Gradually, he put more distance between them until he looked back and found he had taken a bend in the trail that left the wagon out of his view.

Suddenly, out of nowhere it seemed, they came.

There were only four of them, but too many for him to take on by himself.

Three Indians jumped him while a fourth sat his horse and watched. Tom scuffled trying to break free, but one Indian locked his arms around his chest from the back. A second grasped his ankles and brought him to the ground. The third put a knife to his throat.

To Tom's surprise, the Indian sitting on the horse spoke broken English.

"I speak your tongue. What have you done with my sister?"

"Your sister? What are you talking about?" Tom flinched as the knife point pricked his neck.

"White Dove."

Tom ran the information over in his head. *So, there is another relative of the baby. An uncle. He appeared to be a Chief, now.*

"Your sister died of the disease. We buried her."

The Indian has followed us a long ways. It isn't likely he'll accept her fate and go home, Tom suspected. He noted a slight change of expression at the word "disease." Indians feared nothing much more than a sickness they couldn't see or fight.

"Bad medicine. The whole town died of it," Tom emphasized. "We may be carrying it with us, for all we know." He gritted his teeth and pulled his head as far away from the knife blade as he could.

The Indian on the horse said something in his native language and the other three Indians pulled Tom to his feet and stepped back.

Tom stumbled and acted as if he suffered the effects of illness.

The three Indians looked at the one on the horse, not sure whether to continue guarding the man or turn away from him and run.

White Dove's brother reached out with his spear and

held Tom at a distance while the other men retreated.

It was clear they did not want to catch whatever illness the white man might carry.

"The papoose?"

"Well, we're not sure if she's going to make it, either. White Dove was already dead when we found her. The babe got a rough start. Sickness or not, she's going to take a lot of care to try to save her."

White Dove's brother seemed to be mulling the existing situation over in his mind.

Tom could hear the wagon closing the distance behind them.

The Indian didn't have much time to decide his fate.

Tom had no doubt, had the baby been a boy, White Dove's brother would claim him and go, if he were not too afraid of the sickness. *Since, it is a girl—we'll have to see how deep his commitment goes. He is probably already angry that his sister went off with a white man.*

"Sickness come. Everyone sick. White Dove went to teepee with tall steeple. All die, except me and—" he swung his arm toward the other three Indians. "Sick, very sick. But we live. Come for White Dove when sickness gone. Whites have it. We burn white man's town. Papoose sick?"

"She's not doing too good yet. Can't say if she'd bring the sickness back down on you or not." Tom hoped, if there was enough fear of the disease, he could keep the baby from being taken back to an Indian camp where she might die. *What would White Dove's brother know about taking care of an infant? If everyone has died, except him and the remnants of his small band, who would care for her?*

"Look, if you let us go on, I'll see to it the papoose is taken care of. I'll do everything I can to see that she survives." Tom raised himself up tall and strong against the point of the Indian's spear.

I have to convince the Indian to let us pass and take the baby with us. He could hear the wagon getting closer now. The Indian would have to make a quick decision. Tom felt the blade on the spear waver against his chest.

"Brave Eagle," the Indian said.

"Brave Eagle, if you let us take care of her, I'll see that she knows who her family is. If she makes it, she can come back to her people later, if she has a mind to."

Brave Eagle looked toward the intensifying sound of the approaching wagon. It was clear he knew he would soon be outnumbered with guns. The other three Indians moved away to crouch in the brush.

"What's it going to be, Brave Eagle? She goes with you, to die, or goes with us to live?"

Brave Eagle reached up and lifted a necklace of beads and bear claws from his neck. He tossed it to Tom and dropped his spear point toward the dirt below his feet.

"It is a good omen. The medicine man blessed it to heal me. Keep it for her."

He rapidly turned his horse by its mane and kicked his moccasins into the animal's flanks.

Tom broke into a heavy sweat. He felt it trickle from

between his shoulder blades down his spine like a cold finger. He put his hand to his neck and found blood on his fingers when he withdrew them. It dried quickly and he felt again to make sure his throat wasn't cut.

He mounted his horse and rode toward the wagon.

~ * ~

When they reached Waco, Tom instructed Joe to bring the wagon alongside the prison wall. There, they unloaded the men and headed them into the compound. Once the prisoners were secure in their cells, Tom returned to the Ranger's office and handed in his badge.

"Hate to have you leave," his superior told him.

"It's time I make another life for myself."

"Keep your badge for good luck. If you ever want to go back to work, you know where to find us."

Tom shook the man's hand and went back outside where Maria and Reyes waited.

The baby lay quietly in its basket, which sat on the boardwalk at Maria's feet.

Maria's horse was tied to the hitching rail alongside where Reyes' sat on his large black mount. He sat stiffly in the saddle waiting for her to join him.

"What are you going to do if you get back there, and she doesn't marry you?" Maria asked Tom as she looked up at him from her position where she squatted next to the baby on the boardwalk.

He heard a twinge in her voice. *Is it jealousy? Is it irritation that he would even presume a woman, which was nearly a stranger to him, would consider making a home and a family with him?*

"Well, then, I guess I'll either have a child to raise on my own, or have to come looking for you to help me," he said with a twinkle in his eye.

Maria blushed.

Tom got on his horse and loosened his vest.

Maria stuffed the flour sack with the baby's things inside one of his saddlebags. Then, she took the infant from her bed. She snuggled her close to her breast and spoke a few words in Spanish to her before kissing her on the forehead.

"You can probably find us around the Moriarty area if you ever get back this way," Tom told Reyes. "When she's old enough, I'll tell her about you, Maria."

Tears welled in Maria's eyes as she handed the little bundle up to Tom.

He cradled her a few moments in his arm, then snuggled her inside his vest and buttoned the front to keep her secure, leaving his hands free to control his horse.

"*Adios, amigo*," Reyes said as Tom reined his horse away from the hitching rail.

Maria untied the reins of her horse from the rail, and swung up onto her saddle, catching her skirt between her legs to secure it from billowing while she rode. The horse sidestepped to follow Tom.

Maria pulled it back alongside Reyes.

"Until we meet again," Maria called after them.

~ * ~

When Tom arrived in Moriarty, he tied his horse in

front of the boarding house and carefully dismounted with his tiny bundle secure inside his vest. Fortunately, the baby slept peacefully and he moved toward the front door and knocked.

Mrs. Swartz answered his rap.

"Shelia and Elias, are they still here?"

"Yes, but they're getting ready to leave town in a day or two."

"Leave?"

"Yes. Shelia has a job waiting over in Albuquerque. She and Elias are planning to go there. I've written a letter of recommendation to one of my friends there to try to help them get accommodations."

Tom felt his heart sink. *Am I too late?*

"But, they are here now?"

"Yes. Come in. I'll go call Shelia." Mrs. Swartz looked at the rounded lump of Tom's vest and wondered what he carried there. She kept her silence. *None of my business*, she told herself.

Elias came running down the hall from the back room of the house.

"Mr. Tom. Mr. Tom," he called.

Tom squatted down, being careful not to disturb the baby and held his arms out both to greet the boy and to keep him from crashing into his chest.

"I'm happy to see you, too, Elias."

Shelia walked up behind them and Tom stood back up.

"Is there somewhere we can talk?"

"Yes. But, what is so serious that we can't talk here?"

"Elias, why don't you visit with this nice lady while your ma and I go for a walk?" Tom nodded toward Mrs. Swartz. That is all right, isn't it?" He wanted both women's permission.

Tom handed Elias a small wooden toy train engine he had carried in his pocket, to ease the boy's anxiety at being left behind.

Tom opened the door and let Shelia walk through first. He felt the baby stir against his chest. She let out a small whimper.

Shelia looked at him with curiosity.

Once they were outside, Tom reached into his vest and took the baby out. He handed her to Shelia.

"What a sweet little baby," Shelia said, trying to comprehend where and how he had come by the child.

"Her parents died and she had no one else to take care of her. I figured, if you would have us, we could get married and make the four of us a family."

"Tom Jennings. We hardly know each other."

"I know that. But, I'll work hard to take care of all of you. People have gotten married for lesser reasons than we have. The baby needs parents and a home. You and Elias need a home, too. Hell, um, pardon me, I'm tired of riding herd on outlaws and never sleeping in the same bunk twice. I want a home, too. Figure, we all want the same thing. I promise I'll be a good father to Elias, too.

Shelia saw the baby open her eyes and then scrunch them tight as she frowned.

"I've made other plans, Tom. Not that you aren't a

good man—I know you are. It's just, well, you really took me by surprise."

"You don't have to answer right now. Consider it, will you?"

"Of course," Shelia ran the proposal over in her mind. She did have a job waiting and it was a chance to make a better life for her and Elias. Tom was a decent man and she wanted someone to make a home with—someone that could show Elias how to ride and do man things. It would be good to get him out of living in boarding houses and into a more normal life.

"In the meantime, would you mind looking after the baby? Just for a couple of days?"

Tom had ulterior motives in his own mind. He thought getting Shelia involved with the child would improve his chances of convincing her to marry him. He didn't realize her heart was tugging her in two directions. One to make a new life on her own, and the other to follow the stirrings in her heart that she felt when he was around. She had led a hard life. Men had taken advantage of her and now here was one willing to marry her and make a life with her. How could she resist? Still, she kept her answer to herself until she could think clearly again.

"I'll take care of the baby until it is time for Elias, and me, to catch the stage for Albuquerque. I'll give you my answer then."

Tom turned to his horse and retrieved the baby's things from his saddlebag. All the while, he instructed Shelia on how to care for the infant.

Shelia laughed lightly.

"Tom Jennings, don't you think I've done this before?"

"Yes. It's just—I figure we best keep her on the same routine so she doesn't get upset. I'll see if I can get a room here for the night and check in with you as often as possible. I want to ride out to the Westerman's house tomorrow. I thought I'd ask Molly if we could get married there, if you say 'yes', of course."

Shelia smiled.

"You make it hard to resist. How could a woman say 'no' to a man that would bring her a present like this and then ask her to marry him? I'll talk to Elias tonight."

Tom followed Shelia back into the boarding house where Elias sat on the floor running his train engine around the circle of the crocheted rug using its multi-colored lines for track.

He looked up.

"Elias, I want you to see who Tom brought with him. Isn't it adorable?"

Elias peered at the baby briefly, then dropped back down on the floor.

"Is it a boy or girl?" Mrs. Swartz asked.

"Girl," Tom said.

"Oh, do let me hold her," Mrs. Swartz said to Shelia.

Shelia relinquished the bundle into her arms.

"She'll be staying with me a couple of days. Tom would like a room again for a night or so as well."

"I'll be right glad to have him. You can take the same one you used last time, Mr. Jennings."

"Thank you. I'll go see to my horse and be back in a bit. Would you like to ride along, Elias?"

"Oh, Ma, can I?" Elias became excited and pleaded with Shelia.

"Yes, but you must do exactly as Mr. Jennings tells you."

"Oh, I will. I will."

"We'll only be a few minutes," Tom told Shelia. He reached over and ran his finger across the baby's cheek. It was soft to his rough skin.

"I'll be right back," he promised Shelia and the baby.

~ * ~

Early the next day, Tom rode out to the Westerman homestead alone.

He had asked Shelia to be thinking of a name for the baby and, he intended to ask Molly and Trace to let them be married at their house, if Shelia did agree to the ceremony.

Not being a patient man, he hated the indecisiveness he was caught up in. Yet he sensed, if he rushed Shelia, her answer might not be the one he wanted. He called on all the reserves he had to maintain his faltering patience. Remembering the time he had nearly died and Doc Landry wouldn't let him rush his recovery, he tried to tell himself this was just as important a turning point in his life. It could have all been over then and he wouldn't even have this chance at raising a family.

Most of the Westermans stood on the front porch watching him ride in and he felt a stir of excitement. He and Shelia could have a home like this of their own someday. He hungered to live a settled life. He only hoped she longed for the same.

Trace came from the barn toward the front yard of the house. He recognized Tom and raised his hand in greeting.

At his gesture, the children ran forward, excited to have a visitor.

"Tom. Good to see you. Get down off you horse and rest a spell. Andy, take his horse and water it. Put it out to pasture with the others. Tom'll be staying for dinner."

Tom didn't protest, so Andy took hold of the bridle and waited for Tom to dismount.

Tom removed his hat once he stood on the ground.

"Good day, Molly. You're looking right fit."

"Thank you, Tom. We're doing well. You will stay for dinner?"

"Yes, thank you. I have some things to talk to you and Trace about."

"Well, come on in, Tom," Trace said as he slapped Tom on the shoulder then remembered the wound and hoped he had tapped him high enough that he hadn't caused him pain. "Didn't know when we'd ever see you again."

"Take the children and play, Rosie," Molly urged, hoping to keep them out of the house temporarily so the adults could have a conversation without the children hearing.

The two younger ones stared at the stranger.

Seth noticed the pearl-handled pistol and remembered the kick it had when he'd taken it while Tom was injured. He'd tried to convince Molly he had learned his lesson about messing with guns, then. He knew Molly still didn't trust him.

She saw him looking at the pistol and gave him a stare that told him not to mess around.

He ducked his head and skipped off the porch behind Rosie and the younger children before Molly could lecture him in front of Mr. Jennings.

"Have a seat," Trace said when the adults entered the kitchen.

"Would you like a cold drink, Tom?" Molly asked. She could tell Tom had news to share and she didn't want to postpone the excitement any longer than necessary. But, she had to be polite and offer.

"No. Thanks, Molly. I'm fine."

"So your trip to Waco was uneventful?" Trace asked.

Tom unfolded his story to Trace and Molly, ending with the fact that he had asked Shelia to marry him.

"We'd be happy to have you folks get married here," Molly said. "Wouldn't we, Trace?"

"Sure would. After what we've all been through together, it's only neighborly." Trace went on to tell Tom about a small plot of land that was available a few miles down the road toward Estancia.

"It's got a tiny cabin on it. It isn't much, but it would be shelter while you build something larger. All the neighbors would be happy to help."

"I appreciate that. Now, I have to get Shelia to say 'yes'."

"I can hardly wait to meet her," Molly said. "It will be nice to have another woman to talk to. It's so seldom there's anyone nearby."

~ * ~

Three days later, Molly was busy preparing the house for a visit from Tom, Shelia and the children to discuss wedding plans.

She sang happily as she busied herself with the simple housework.

"Seth, take the broom and go beat the tansy and mint bushes. Take Emmy with you. It's time she watched and learned what to do."

Teaching Emmy to sweep the bushes was bittersweet for Seth. It had been his job, for the last three years, to take the broom and hit the clumps of bushes that grew alongside the doors of the house. Bruising the tansy leaves emitted an odor, into the air, that made the flies stay away from the doors and, therefore, out of the house. The scent of mint, also from its tender snapped twigs when hit with the broom, made the house smell fresh when company arrived.

Now, he knew he would soon be handing the job over to Emmy. It fell to the youngest child to beat the bushes. It was a simple chore that the youngest would usually do with glee until they got tired of it. Then, they would simply wait until the next child became old enough to inherit the position. In a way, he would be glad to hand the job over to Emmy, but it also meant he was growing up and would no longer get preferential treatment from the adults. He didn't want to be considered a baby, yet he felt a loss at growing away from his younger years.

Twenty-five

The morning of Tom and Shelia's wedding came on a hot summer day. It seemed like preparations had been underway for days now. Trace and Andy had cleared the widest section in the barn for a dance floor to celebrate after the brief ceremony.

Molly and Rosie set a trellis Trace had build in the midst of the red hollyhocks and wove the stalks through the fine lattice on its sides, curving the flower stalks through the holes until they filled the crest of the trellis.

The red blooms were like miniature ballet dresses poking their fabric through the whitewashed slats.

Trace and Andy approached the area where Molly fussed with the tall stalks, trying to make certain all the spaces were filled.

Trace stood studying the archway as she worked.

"The babies are napping," Molly told him. Seth and Crazy Leg are supposed to be watching them."

"I didn't think you'd want them out in the midst of your flowers. You picked a good time to work on this— whatever it is."

"It's an idea I read about in one of the women's

magazines from back east. Getting married isn't just standing up and saying 'I do,' anymore."

"We've got the barn floor ready for dancing. I even made some benches for people to sit on."

"How many guests do you think we'll have?" Molly considered the preparations of the food.

"Not too many. Tom doesn't know many folks around here. The sheriff and his wife, I'm sure. Becky and her parents. Doc Landry and his wife. Maybe a few more."

"The Johnsons," Molly added. "Andy, I want you to ride into Moriarty and make arrangements with that photographer fellow that took your picture when you and Comet won that race. You can invite him and ask him to take a picture of Tom and Shelia and their family after the preacher blesses them. It would be nice for them to be able to see it years down the road when their wedding is only a memory." Already Molly was forming an image, in her mind, of the new family in front of her prized flowers.

She still remembered when she fell in love with Trace. Their vows had been said in front of a few friends in Moriarty, more as a formality—a way for them to get on with their lives as man and wife. A widow with three step-children, she remembered feeling amazed that a man could love her and take on a family of that size. There had been no celebration afterwards, just a return to the homestead but she couldn't have been happier. That night, when the children were asleep, Trace had made love to her for the first time.

Not a virgin, having been married to the children's father, Molly remembered the sweet pleasure of someone that truly loved her expressing himself with his body.

Later, upon reflection, she compared the two men that had shared her bed. With one, she had known ecstasy, with the other, only duty. She felt a thrill within her body and looked into Trace's eyes.

He smiled at her with a knowing look that only comes from the melding of two hearts.

She felt her cheeks warm and smiled back.

Even now, they shared elation when they were alone together. They had made two babies together. Two children she had never thought she would have. The hunger for a child of her own, which had raged within her body, was sated by Trace's love.

She thought about the sweet smell of Emmy's hair when the sun warmed it and she laid her cheek against her head. She thought about the tussle Jacob put up when she tried to snuggle him close and catch a whiff of his freshly washed curls. *He is so like his father, no one, or nothing, was going to hold him down unless he wanted it to.*

Today was a happy occasion.

Trace thought about the last time there had been a gathering at the homestead and thanked God that Molly had survived.

Seth came from the house lugging Jacob in his arms. Emmy followed, clinging to his pant leg.

Molly stopped working on the trellis arch and lifted Emmy into her arms. Trace put his arm around both of them and kissed Molly on the cheek.

Emmy looked up with expectation for her kiss.

Molly laughed.

"We're going to have to watch this one. She'll be expecting attention from everyone."

"And, she'll probably get it." Trace spoke lovingly.

Seth handed Jacob to Rosie.

"Someone's coming!" Seth ran to look around the house for the first guests.

"It's the Doc," he called back.

Molly quickly handed Emmy to Trace and brushed the palms of her hands across her apron, gathering the fabric up and wiping the stain from the flower stems off as best she could.

Molly, Trace and the children went to greet their guests.

Seth took Nellie's halter and waited for Doc and his wife to climb down from the buggy. When they had removed containers of food and a wedding gift, Seth led the horse to a spot near the watering trough where he could tie the horse within reach of the liquid.

"I'd unhook her," Doc said, "but I never know when someone'll come looking for my help."

"Molly, it's good to see you," Mrs. Landry said as they went to take the food inside the house.

"Thank you, so much, for helping ne with the food," Molly said as she relieved Mrs. Landry of one of the baskets in the kitchen.

"Of course. It was fun making something different. My sister and her family will be here soon. I swear her baby is growing up so fast. Like your Emmy. It's hard to believe they're becoming little girls instead of babies."

Molly remembered the times she had traded Mrs. Johnson favors for dairy products before she and Trace married. She remembered the day Rosie had carried Callie back from the Johnson's homestead and the cat became a good reason for Mrs. Johnson to send excess milk home with the family.

"Your sister has been a good neighbor," Molly said.

"She's appreciated your teaching her youngun's."

"And I appreciate Doc saving my life."

"That was God's doin'. Doc said so, himself. There was nothing he could do."

"And we thank God everyday, too!"

A touch of uneasiness crossed Molly's mind as she thought about taking Rosie to see Doc and discuss her concerns with him. *How much does Doc tell his wife? Does Mrs. Landry know about Rosie's peculiarities?* She prayed Rosie wouldn't act up today and embarrass the family with her strange behavior.

"More wagons coming," Seth ran into the house to announce. "Looks like a whole parcel of 'em, Ma."

"Good. We can use some company to share the celebration with. Did you see if Mr. Jennings was driving one of them?"

"No. But, there's a fancy carriage in the front. It's all decorated up. Bet that's him."

Seth was so excited he couldn't wait to bounce back outside the house and greet the guests. Crazy Leg bounded up and down with excitement. It seemed the gaiety was contagious.

"Quickly, Seth. Grab the broom and go sweep the bushes again!" Molly, concerned that her house be perfect, called after him but he was already too far away to hear amidst the clatter of the incoming wagons.

"I'll do it, Ma," Rosie said as she came through the doorway with Emmy's hand in hers. "Pa has Jacob. We can do that, can't we Emmy?"

Emmy rushed for the broom and dragged it by its long handle with the straw head in tow.

"Here, let me help you," Rosie reached to grab the handle before Emmy knocked a lamp out of its bracket on the wall. Callie chased after the broom straws, when Rosie corrected its direction, attacking them as if she was chasing a rat.

Molly, wiping her hands on her apron before she removed it, went with Mrs. Landry to greet the guests.

Outside, in the front yard, she saw Trace holding Jacob as he shook hands with Tom Jennings in the front carriage.

Next to Tom, on one side, was a young boy. On the other side sat Shelia holding the baby in her arms.

Seth and Crazy Leg stood nearby. A shyness showed on Seth's tanned face but Crazy Leg couldn't resist the excitement and darted from one side of the carriage to the other.

Behind the first carriage, a short line of buckboards and buggies filed from the main road.

"Go ahead and pull your carriage up alongside the Doc's over there," Trace told Tom.

Andy and Doc came from the open barn door. Doc waved to Tom, intending the greeting for the rest of the group as well.

Andy rushed ahead to help park the wagons.

Pastor Jones rode up on his horse and dismounted.

The yard was a conglomeration of wagons and horses and Andy opened the corral to find space to keep the unhitched animals.

The excitement was too much for Crazy Leg. He jumped and dodged horse hooves until he jogged the wrong way and was clipped by a hoof.

"*Yip!*"

"Crazy Leg! Get out of here," Andy called to him. "Seth, come get your dog!"

Elias was on the ground now and moved to say "hello" to Seth.

"Some dog. Wish I had one."

"Elias, you stay clean, now, you hear?" Shelia was concerned that he might forget the importance of their visit and get dirty before the ceremony. She handed the baby to Tom. Trace, Jacob still in his one arm, reached up to help her down from the carriage with his other hand.

She wore a tan dress, a shade darker than cream and looked striking. He could see where Tom might get wrapped up in a woman like this. She looked good all gussied up.

"Good to see you, again, Shelia," Trace said. "Molly's real excited about the wedding."

Shelia blushed. Had Tom told them her background? Would they disapprove of her, if they knew? Somehow she sensed the Westerman's were not a judging couple. They had had their own trials, according to what Tom had told her. Life was tough. You had to do what you needed to in order to survive.

"Thank you. I'm sure we'll all be good friends. It's nice to see you again, too."

Seth reached down to pat Crazy Leg on the head.

"Maybe someday you will. Come on," he said to Elias. "I gotta get the dog away before he gets into some more trouble."

Shelia looked after the boys with dismay as Tom handed the baby back to her.

"They'll be fine," Tom assured her when he saw her concern.

A small knot of people gathered around the bride and groom, now, and Shelia edged closer to Tom.

"Pastor Jones," Tom greeted the minister. "This is Shelia. We'd like you to bless the baby, too. We've picked a name for her."

"What a glorious day! It is wonderful to be bringing God's blessings for a happy occasion. How do you do, Shelia?"

"Fine, thank you, Pastor."

"We're grateful you could come," Tom said.

Introductions were made all around and people broke off into twos and threes to help with preparations or join in conversation.

~ * ~

"Are you sure we can go into the loft?" Elias asked as he followed Seth up the ladder and through the opening.

"Sure. I do it all the time."

Elias was apprehensive. He had never been out of Moriarty and the barn seemed ominous to him.

A chicken clucked and flew away toward the opening for loading the hay into the loft.

"What was that?" Elias asked anxiously.

"Don't be a fraidy cat. It was only a chicken. Don't you know what a chicken is? Eggs come from chickens."

"Oh." Elias didn't want to admit that he didn't know.

"Where'd you think they came from?" Seth was

obviously the more experienced child.

"I don' know. Never thought about it."

"Come on. I've got some stuff hid up here we can play with."

Elias did as he was told, staying far enough behind Seth that he wouldn't get kicked in the face by the other boy's feet when they climbed the ladder. Once they were in the loft he looked down through the hole where the ladder stood. It seemed a long way down and he felt dizzy.

"Come on."

The dust in the hay made it hard for Elias to breathe. He wanted fresh air but didn't know how to get it in this room where sunlight filtered through a light fog of dust.

Once they reached the corner of the barn loft, Seth moved hay away from where the walls came together in the corner and reached for his treasure. A small sack was hidden there and Seth pulled it out to show Elias what it contained.

They sat cross-legged on the floor while Seth exposed his prizes, one-by-one.

"This's the aggie I won a bunch of marbles with at school."

He handed the large round glass-looking marble to Elias.

Elias held it up in his fingers and looked at the light through it. Then, he put it back in Seth's hand.

"And, here's some old rattles Pa cut off a snake once." Seth shook the rattles and he heard Crazy Leg whine below him. The dog, unable to climb the ladder, waited at the bottom for the boys to return from their adventure.

Next, Seth pulled a rusty pistol from his sack. It was small, not much larger than Elias's hand.

"Wow! Where'd you get that?"

"I found it when we were in town one time." Seth rubbed it across his pants leg. The small derringer appeared beyond the capability of functioning. Seth cocked the hammer back.

"If I had a bullet for it, I'd show you how it works." He spoke proudly. He had always liked guns even if they had gotten him in a lot of trouble in the past. He didn't see how this one could do any harm. It was so small. *How could it hurt anybody?*

"Don't you dare tell anyone! Ma'd have my hide if she found out I had it."

Elias nodded his head in agreement, his mouth wide open in awe. He had never seen such interesting things.

There was a noise below and Seth hurriedly replaced the items in their bag and put it back in its corner. He quickly covered the bag with the loose hay.

"Shh. Hide behind that pile of hay over there," Seth pointed out. "I'm right behind you."

Slowly, Rosie came up the stairs. Her movement was like the slinking of a cat and she moved across the loft on all fours.

Elias and Seth watched from where they had secluded themselves.

"What's she doin'?" Elias asked in a whisper.

"I don't know." Seth had never seen Rosie look the way she did now. It was almost as if her ears had grown points and her eyes were closed to slits like he had seen Callie's when she purred contentedly alongside the stove.

Rosie moved to a pile of hay and wound herself around in a circle until she had a bed of hay packed to curl up in. Once she was satisfied with her bed, she curled tight with her knees pulled to her chest and went to sleep.

"What do we do now?" Elias asked.

"Get out of here without waking her up, I guess. Be very quiet and tiptoe away. Follow me."

Seth felt uneasy. He was disturbed by Rosie's actions. *Perhaps she just needed a nap. But, why did she go about it in such a strange way?* He puzzled whether he should tell Ma what they had seen. He knew Rosie would call him a 'tattletale,' again, if he did.

When the boys and Crazy Leg reached the cluster of people standing beside the trellis in front of the kitchen window, Seth decided not to mention Rosie's strange actions and nudged Elias to tell him to keep quiet as well.

Elias nodded. It was the first time he had had a friend and, even though Seth was older than he, he wanted to see that they remained close.

"Elias! Where have you been?" Shelia handed the baby to Molly and turned to brush the hay away from Elias's clothes. Molly looked at Seth and he began brushing away the telltale hay as well.

"Seth, you shouldn't have taken Elias into the barn before the ceremony. Shelia wants him to look good for their picture."

"Sorry, Ma," Seth hung his head and studied the toes of Andy's old shoes he wore that were polished to a shine.

"No harm done," Shelia announced. "Now, you stay here, Elias, until we're through. After the picture you can change into your other clothes and go play."

Rosie came from the barn, brushing the back of her skirt as she walked.

"I think it's time we had the wedding vows before the babies get cranky and the littler kids get dirty," Molly suggested.

"Pastor Jones," Tom called to the preacher. "We're ready."

Everyone gathered around Tom, Shelia, and Elias. They stood in front of the arch. Molly continued to hold the baby until the preacher announced Tom and Sheila, "Man and Wife."

Tom leaned down and kissed Shelia lightly on the lips.

"That's a promise of more to come," Tom whispered in her ear.

Molly hugged Shelia and handed the baby back to her.

"We're here today, also, to bless this baby," Pastor Jones said, "and, to give her a name. Tom?"

Tom and Shelia turned toward the preacher with the baby. Elias looked up with expectation, waiting for God, or the preacher, to reach his hand down and pat his head.

"Lord, bless these children," Pastor Jones said. "Bless Elias and—"

"Eliza White Dove Jennings," Tom said. He'd explain her name to his friends later when the time was right but, for now, Eliza would do.

"—Eliza," Pastor Jones said. "Lord, bless us all in this, one of our happier times. Amen."

A chorus of "Amens" followed. All of the people, including the newly wed couple, knew tougher times might lie ahead. They would take what joy they could when it presented itself.

The sheriff, Doc Landry, and several other men stepped forward to congratulate the couple. The men slapped Tom on the back and, soon, moved him away from the women toward the barn.

Shelia looked after him, knowing they would reconnect later. Tom looked back and raised his hand in a gesture to let her know he would return as soon as he could.

"Got a jug in the back of my wagon, if anybody's interested," Mr. Johnson told the men. A few of them wandered off toward the wagon to drink the liquor. Others stood in a circle and discussed the fact that Tom was no longer a "free man."

There were different takes on whether his life would be better or worse. Most of them agreed, he couldn't want much more.

Elias crawled into the buggy and retrieved his play clothes while Seth shed his hand-me-down shoes in favor of running barefoot.

The women went to set up the refreshments and sounds of a fiddle warming up in the barn floated through the air.

Andy sought Becky out amidst the women setting up refreshments and motioned for her to come to the back door of the barn.

"What do you want, Andy?"

"I want to talk to you. Will you come with me?"

"I don't think we have much to say to each other. Please, don't spoil the party."

"Then, come with me so I can explain."

Becky looked around at her mother. She wondered if she should listen to Andy or stand her ground. She wanted to ignore him, but her heart wouldn't let her.

"All right. But, I warn you, I might not like what you have to say."

"Just hear me out."

The two of them walked toward the windmill. Andy sat down on the edge of the watering trough where it filled from the pipe Trace had installed. He motioned for Becky to sit, too.

"What you thought you saw that night in the barn was none of my doing."

"You two looked pretty cozy to me."

"You know we were helping Maria. Whatever feelings she might have had toward me, I didn't feel the same. Shucks, she was some older than me."

"She certainly acted like she knew what she was doing."

"I told you, if she liked me, it wasn't my fault. I was doing what Ma said—teaching her how to milk. Too bad Bossy can't talk. She'd tell you the same thing."

"Well—"

"Anyway, Maria's gone back home to Mexico. There's nothing to worry about now. Even if she was here, I promise you, I wouldn't be taking up with her."

Becky picked at a thread in the seam of her dress.

Andy edged his hand along the rim of the watering trough until it touched Becky's fingers.

He hesitated.

Becky, uncertain whether to trust him, again, or not, studied the closeness of their hands. She looked away and could see some of the men at the back of Mr. Johnson's wagon, hear the music coming from the barn and smell the sent of honeysuckle wrapped around one leg of the nearby support for the windmill.

Dusk was falling. It would soon be dark.

She loved Andy, she knew, even though they were both young. "Puppy love," her pa had said. But, she didn't believe him. She felt it was real. Why else had the pain hurt so much in her heart when she saw him with his arms around that girl?

But, she was gone, now. How much threat could she be hundreds of miles away in another country?

Becky edged the tips of her fingers toward Andy's and he grasped her hand in his when they touched.

"Can't we patch this up and go on from where we were, Becky?"

"It will take time, Andy. How will I know if I can ever trust you again?"

Andy swallowed hard. She still didn't believe he was totally innocent.

"I promise, Becky. You will never find me in a bad position like that again."

He raised her hand to his lips and kissed it barely above the knuckles. He stood up and tugged, lightly, on her arm to lead her toward the hops strung in rows nearby. There, with the dim light and tall vines secluding them, no one near the house and barn could see them. When they reached a row where he was sure no one could watch, he pulled Becky close and touched his lips to her cheek.

She looked up at him with desire in her eyes. She so wanted to believe him—so wanted to love him—that she relented and released her anger and thoughts of betrayal.

She moved her lips to meet his and they wrapped in an embrace.

~ * ~

"Look what I found, Elias," Seth reached his hand out to show the other boy when they were behind the barn.

He opened his palm and flattened it out, exposing a small twenty-two caliber bullet.

"What is it?" Elias, sheltered from living in a boarding house all his life, found the piece of metal interesting but had no idea what it was for or what it did.

"It's a bullet. I think it will fit in the gun I showed you. Pa bought Andy a new twenty-two rifle to shoot snakes with. When I saw the bullets, I thought they'd fit the gun I found." Seth pulled the rusty weapon from his pants pocket. "I went back and got it. But, I waited to see if it would work until we could try it together."

Seth didn't tell Elias that he had already had experience with guns. Once when he had caught his big toe in Ma's rifle trigger and once when he had sneaked Tom's pearl-handled revolver out to try it. He clutched his fist back, tight over the bullet, when Crazy Leg's curiosity made him jump up to see if Seth held a treat in his hand.

"It's just one little shell. It can't do much harm. I know enough to point it away from us."

Elias became excited by the find. He had never gotten to satisfy his own curiosity about the world, and, now, it seemed that life had all kinds of interesting things to learn. And Seth might be a good teacher.

The commotion inside the barn where the adults danced and refreshments were being served covered any noise the boys made so Seth was not afraid to load and fire the derringer.

Elias looked eagerly down the barrel while Seth pushed

the bullet into the hole. Seth turned the gun away.

"You can't be in front of it."

"Oh, all right."

"Remember, I said it has to be pointed away."

"Yeah, I remember."

"That means you can't get in front of it, either."

Seth fumbled with the bullet trying to get the casing to pass by a chunk of rust.

Inside the barn, Molly was dipping punch into cups for the guests. She scooped liquid from the bowl and poured it into a cup.

The derringer's firing was a slight whisper, its sound covered by the music and voices inside the barn.

Molly looked down when she heard glass shattering and saw punch running from the side of the bowl where chunks of glass had blown away.

"What?"

The liquid sprayed over her dress and she dropped the cup she had filled.

People scattered away from the refreshment table and Trace sprinted for the door.

"Stay down, everybody, until I find out what's going on!"

As he reached the open door, Seth, Elias and Crazy Leg ran by him.

"Hey! Stop! What's going on?"

Seth stopped so quickly, Elias and Crazy Leg ran into him and the three of them ended up in a heap at Trace's feet.

"Seth! What have you been up to?"

Knowing he looked guilty from trying to escape, Seth

got up on his feet and hung his head.

"I—I had an old gun I found."

"Give it to me."

"I dropped it."

"Then *you* fired the shot?"

"Yes."

Trace looked angrier than Seth had ever seen him.

"What the hell are we going to do with you, Seth? One of these days you're going to kill someone messing around with guns. You don't know what you're doing and I think you might be too young to learn."

The sheriff, who had joined Trace in search of the location of the shot, stepped up to the boys.

"I could arrest him and lock him up in the jail in town, if you want me to do that, Trace," the sheriff said with seriousness.

Seth felt like he was going to be sick and fought back tears.

"That might be a good idea, Sheriff. This boy's got to learn a lesson."

"It's all right, folks," Trace turned and called back over his shoulder to the revelers inside the barn. "I think we caught the culprits right here. It was only the kids messing where they shouldn't be."

Shelia and Tom hurried to Trace's side.

"Elias! What have you done?"

"It wasn't his fault, Ma'am. I was showing him something and it went off. I didn't mean no harm."

"Any. You didn't mean any harm," Molly corrected automatically.

"What are we going to do with you, Seth?" Trace

studied the boy before him. They had faced his curiosity about guns in the past. He thought that was behind them. Some way, they had to get through to the boy that they were dangerous. He had to leave them alone.

Molly, letting Trace handle the situation, tried to put her guests back at ease. Some of the men chuckled about the punch bowl and Molly's shocked look when it sprang a leak. The women, more concerned at what might have happened, fussed a bit, but soon turned their attention back to the celebration.

"What if the bullet had hit you instead of the punch bowl, Molly? What if it had hit someone else?" A couple of the women fussed and postulated.

Shaken, but calm, now that the crisis was over, Molly tried to reassure the other women.

"No harm done," Molly told Mrs. Landry. She didn't mention that her mind was racing with thoughts that one of the guests, or babies, might have been hit instead of the punch bowl. *Thank God for that! The punch bowl can be done without.*

"Rest assured, Seth will be dealt with!"

"You're right. No one is hurt. Don't be too harsh on the boy, although, I do understand that he has to be taught not to mess with things that could hurt someone," Mrs. Johnson commiserated with Molly.

"You're right. So far, we've been lucky that he hasn't hurt anyone or himself. We can't watch him all the time. How on earth are we ever going to get him to stop fussing with guns?"

"I surely don't know."

Becky's mother approached the other two women.

"Perhaps you should have him watch Doc take a bullet out of someone sometime."

"That's a good idea. Maybe it would sink in, then." Molly agreed.

"I'm sure Doc would be glad to oblige," Mrs. Landry said as she overheard the conversation.

The punishment seemed to be settled upon and Becky's mother asked the question she had approached Molly with.

"Have you seen Becky and Andy? I can't seem to find them anywhere."

"I'm sure they're around here, somewhere. How much trouble could they get into here?" But the thought nagged Molly's mind. *Where are they? And, what are they doing?*

Twenty-six

Andy felt life stirring inside his pants, as he held Becky close in the hop vines in the twilight. He hoped Becky didn't feel what he did because he knew he couldn't do anything about it.

They continued to kiss both sensing that it was fueling a fire inside of them. Andy was trying to decide what he should do next, and Becky was trying to decide how far she should let Andy go, when a gruff voice with a heavy accent broke through their heavy breathing.

"*Niño!*"

The man grabbed the two of them. His breath was strong with the scent of onions and alcohol. Jesus pulled them toward the outer edge of the hop vines where he had quietly walked his horse in the cultivated soil.

"Maria is gone. Perhaps I should take your girl with me, instead," Jesus threatened Andy. "Maybe I could trade her for Maria in Mexico. Your *fiesta* goes on. No one would know she was gone for some time."

Molly, with Rosie by her side, was heading toward the house to put the babies to bed when they heard the scream.

Becky, jerked away from Andy by Jesus, shrieked as loudly as she could.

Molly stopped in her tracks.

"Rosie, take the children into the house."

She sprinted back toward the barn.

"Trace! Trace!"

Trace and the sheriff came running toward the door.

"What is it?"

"I heard a scream. I think it might have been Becky."

Becky's mother rushed forward. *What is going on? Surely, Andy wouldn't be responsible for something that would cause Becky to scream. I have always trusted Andy. He was a good boy. I'm sure.*

"Which direction did it come from?" Trace saw the sheriff rush for his horse.

"It sounded like it was over by the windmill."

Trace took off on foot. The sheriff saw the direction he was running and ran his horse ahead.

As the sheriff approached the hops, he saw two figures struggling with a third.

He reined his horse to a stop, throwing soft dirt across them.

Andy was pulling on Jesus' arm in an attempt to get him to release Becky. Becky twisted in Jesus' grip, trying to catch her breath for another scream.

"Hold it there!" The sheriff shouted.

Jesus stopped struggling with the two immediately.

"What's going on here?"

"This is one of Reyes Espiañata's former *vaqueros*. I recognized him. I think he's the one that stole Comet before. He was trying to drag Becky away from me,"

Andy explained.

Becky fell into Andy's arms and sobbed. Her heart beat rapidly against his chest and he vowed he would protect her to his last breath.

"You two go on back to the party. Trace and I'll deal with this kidnapping horse thief."

Trace caught up as Andy and Becky turned to walk away.

"Seems this one can't stay out of trouble. Recognize him, Trace?"

Trace reached forward and tilted the man's face toward the moonlight that now provided a slight glow.

"Sure do. He's the horse thief, all right."

"Then I guess we better tie him up until I can get him back to the jail. Maybe hangin' isn't good enough for him."

Trace didn't think the law would be able to do much with him except take him back to Mexico and turn him loose at the border. The law was less likely to hang a horse thief these days, but he suspected the sheriff wasn't about to tell his prisoner that. Kidnapping was another crime all together. They would have to prove he had taken Maria and that was a Mexico problem. It would be punishment enough, for him, if they turned him over to Reyes Espiañata. Hanging, there, might rid both sides of the problem *vaquero*.

With their prisoner secured to the windmill tower, tied tightly to one leg of the derrick in a sitting position and his feet bound, Trace suggested they return to the celebration, too.

"It's getting late. I'm sure people are going to be

leaving soon."

"Sure you don't want me to take your boy back to town with me just to teach him a lesson?" The sheriff led his horse and walked with Trace as they went back to the barn. Andy kept his arm around Becky as they moved ahead of them.

"I've been thinking about that. I don't think Molly'll like it, and he is a little young but, I intend to teach him how to shoot. Maybe, if he learns how to handle the weapons and how dangerous they can be, he won't have so much curiosity."

"That sounds like a good possibility," the sheriff agreed.

When they reached the barn, Mrs. Waite rushed toward Andy and Becky.

"What on earth is going on, Rebecca?"

Andy released Becky to go to her mother and cry on her shoulder.

The girl was still so wracked with sobs she couldn't speak.

"We were talking out by the garden when a *vaquero* that was hanging around tried to grab Becky," Andy explained.

Mrs. Waite gave him a stern look. She pursed her lips but said nothing.

"Sorry, Mrs. Waite, I didn't think there'd be any harm being out there so close to the house and all."

"We caught him," the sheriff assured her. "He can't hurt anybody now. As soon as this shindig breaks up, I'll stick him in one of the wagons and tie the horse behind so someone can take him back to the jail."

Tom and Shelia came forward.

"I think, maybe, there's been too much excitement for one night," Tom said and turned the slightest pink in the light of the lantern when Trace winked at him.

"Congratulations, Tom. You, too, Shelia. We will all understand, if you're ready to leave," Trace spoke trying to lighten the atmosphere that had descended on the party.

"The kids are already asleep in the buggy and it's been a long day for all of us. We do appreciate your hospitality, Trace. Molly."

"Come and visit us soon," Shelia said as she hugged Molly.

Little by little guests dwindled away and soon Molly and Trace were left with Andy and Rosie to put out the lanterns and join Seth and the babies where they slept in the house.

~ * ~

"Life's not at all like it was when the land was raw and I was a lonesome cowboy," Trace told Molly as he kissed her goodnight.

She hugged him close, feeling his body warm against her nightgown.

It had been a joyous night, except for the two mishaps that plagued them. In the end, everyone was safe and sane. She wondered about Rosie. *Will the day come when Rosie is no longer sane and we have to take her to Las Vegas and lock her away?* Molly wrapped herself tighter around Trace's strong muscles. She didn't want to think that day would ever come. *Hadn't she seemed better lately? Maybe Doc, uneducated in affairs of the mind, is wrong. Perhaps the strange behaviors will go away.*

For tonight, everyone is, at least, safe and happy whether they are sane or not. And, who is to say what sanity is?

Trace, suspecting Molly was worrying, turned and spoke into the darkened room.

"It will be all right, Molly. We've made it through thick and thin, so far. How much more trouble can the world heap upon us?"

"You're right. As long as we've got each other, what more can we ask?"

The couple, still very much in love, kissed once more before drifting off to sleep for the night.

Meet Mary Jean Kelso

Mary Jean Kelso is a correspondent for The Lahontan Valley News, Fernley Today section. Some of her articles are reprinted in The Nevada Appeal. She has been published in many newspapers and magazines, both as a writer and photographer. She was an Assistant Editor for three pharmaceutical magazines before concentrating on fiction. Her books include titles for children, young adults and adults. Previously published novels are *Mystery in Virginia City, A Virginia City Mystery,* and the third printing, *Goodbye is Forever*, recently released. The sequel is *Abducted!* and, the third in the series is *Sierra Summer*. Other titles include *Goodbye, Bodie, The Homesteader*, *Blue Coat* and *The Homesteader's Legacy*.